TREAD

'*Avoid throwing yourself at a man—it's always a mistake.*'
Why should the arrogant Mr Duffy care if Nurse Tiffany Kane ruins her reputation and loses her job because of a silly infatuation? For she loathes *him* with a startling intensity.

*Books you will enjoy
in our Doctor–Nurse series*

ACROSS THE PEARL RIVER by Zara Holman
THE SURGEON'S QUEST by Elizabeth Petty
VISITING CONSULTANT by Betty Neels
FLYAWAY SISTER by Lisa Cooper
TROPICAL NURSE by Margaret Barker
LADY IN HARLEY STREET by Anne Vinton
FIRST-YEAR'S FANCY by Lynne Collins
DESERT FLOWER by Dana James
INDIAN OCEAN DOCTORS by Juliet Shore
CRUISE NURSE by Clare Lavenham
CAPTIVE HEART by Hazel Fisher
A PROFESSIONAL SECRET by Kate Norway
NURSE ON CALL by Leonie Craig
THE GILDED CAGE by Sarah Franklin
A SURGEON CALLED AMANDA by Elizabeth Harrison
VICTORY FOR VICTORIA by Betty Neels
SHAMROCK NURSE by Elspeth O'Brien
ICE VENTURE NURSE by Lydia Balmain
DR VENABLES' PRACTICE by Anne Vinton

TREAD SOFTLY, NURSE

BY
LYNNE COLLINS

MILLS & BOON LIMITED
London · Sydney · Toronto

*First published in Great Britain 1966
by Wright & Brown Ltd*

© Lynne Collins 1966

*Australian copyright 1983
Philippine copyright 1983*

*This edition published 1983 by
Mills & Boon Limited, 15–16 Brook's Mews,
London W1A 1DR*

ISBN 0 263 74326 8

All the characters in this book have no existence outside the imagination of the Author, and have no relation whatsoever to anyone bearing the same name or names. They are not even distantly inspired by any individual known or unknown to the Author, and all the incidents are pure invention.

The text of this publication or any part thereof may not be reproduced or transmitted in any form or by any means, electronic or mechanical, including photocopying, recording, storage in an information retrieval system, or otherwise, without the written permission of the publisher.

This book is sold subject to the condition that it shall not, by way of trade or otherwise, be lent, resold, hired out or otherwise circulated without the prior consent of the publisher in any form of binding or cover other than that in which it is published and without a similar condition including this condition being imposed on the subsequent purchaser.

Set in 11 on 12½ pt Linotron Times
03/0783

*Photoset by Rowland Phototypesetting Ltd
Bury St Edmunds, Suffolk
Made and printed in Great Britain by
Richard Clay (The Chaucer Press) Ltd
Bungay, Suffolk*

CHAPTER ONE

TIFFANY scowled at the sombre sky and the heavy drops of rain, pulled her cloak more warmly about her for protection against the cold and damp and hurried, almost running but not quite, across the small park that nestled between the mass of hospital buildings and the various annexes and departments. She was a small, slight girl with a piquant face and a mass of rich red hair which she kept neatly rolled at the back of her head in deference to the hospital ruling about long hair.

The park was deserted except for herself, another nurse on her way from the hospital to the Nurses' Home that Tiffany had just left and two medical students, so engrossed in their conversation that they seemed to be oblivious to the rain.

Tiffany passed her colleague with no more than a swift, warm smile and a conspiratorial murmur that deplored the weather. There was neither time nor inclination to linger for while Tiffany conceded that she had many faults, unpunctuality was not one of them—mainly because she had learned in the early days of her training that a nurse could not afford to be late on duty. Not only the ward sister or staff nurse but also the colleague she was supposed to relieve would soon give her a sharp set-down if she were even so much as a minute late. So Tiffany had trained herself to be always a few minutes early . . . and as she ran up the wide stone steps and through the massive doors of Main Hall, she glanced instinctively at the big clock above the porter's desk and found that, by hurrying, she had more than ten minutes to spare before she needed to report to Adeline Ward.

Joe, the bulky diabetic porter whose blood pressure always seemed so alarmingly high despite the strict diet and the tablets prescribed for him, gave her his usual broad grin and wheezy greeting. Tiffany's red hair marked her for immediate attention wherever she went and her laughing grey eyes and ready smile made her a universal favourite. Even the starchiest of ward sisters had been known to relent a little when faced with Tiffany Kane's irresistible charm. Perhaps the greatest quality in that charm was Tiffany's own lack of realisation of its devastating effect.

Dr Nigel Goodenough, collecting his mail from the desk, paused to look after the attractive girl as she swept around the corner, her skirts swinging with her brisk steps. 'A sight for sore eyes, Joe,' he commented admiringly.

'A very nice young lady, I'm sure, sir,' Joe agreed heavily. He prided himself on knowing every member of the staff not only by name and sight but also by reputation—and he did not approve of Dr Goodenough whose approach to the opposite sex was a little too fickle and light-hearted.

'Which ward is she on at the moment, Joe?' Nigel did not doubt that the porter would know . . . Joe knew everyone and everything connected with St Christopher's and his information was always reliable.

'Out of your province, sir—Adeline,' the porter told him, almost reluctantly.

Nigel nodded. 'Not one of my wards, as you say . . . never mind. Are those *all* my letters, Joe—it seems quite a batch.'

'Love-letters, I daresay, sir,' he retorted drily.

Nigel grinned. 'Quite possibly,' he agreed and turned away to return to his work with the thought of Tiffany Kane to tantalise him at odd moments during the day . . .

Tiffany mounted the stone staircase, her thoughts busy but not concerned with the young doctor for she had not even noticed him. Ten minutes . . . long enough to slip into Caroline Ward for a few words with Angela. Sister wouldn't mind and Angela would be pleased—and it was practically everyone's business at St Christopher's to ensure that Angela received as much pleasure as possible.

Sister Caroline was nowhere in sight and Staff merely looked up from her work at the desk to smile and nod as Tiffany entered the ward and gestured towards the side ward that Angela occupied.

Angela was twenty-one . . . young and lovely, bright and cheerful and condemned to life in an iron lung since she had been stricken with poliomyelitis two years before. She was dependent on others for every function of daily living . . . except that she could smile and talk, she was as helpless as a baby. Her courage and optimism and complete faith in St Christopher's brightened the lives of everyone around her and Tiffany liked to make a point of visiting her for a few minutes almost every day. Although she might be tired or discouraged by the arduous and demanding work as a nurse, she never left Angela's presence without a renewed conviction that nursing was a worthwhile and very rewarding profession for any girl.

As Tiffany entered and walked to the head of the lung so that she could smile at the reflection of Angela's sweet and pretty face in the mirror poised above her, she said lightly: 'So this is where all the sunshine is today—I should have known!'

Angela's smile was warm with appreciation of the quip and pleasure at seeing Tiffany who had been working on this ward until a few weeks before. They had become very close . . . the nurse and the patient and it had been a wrench for Tiffany to leave Caroline Ward. She had feared that Angela might be upset but the girl had long ago learned to accept that nurses came and went as the authorities decreed.

'Is it a bad day?' Angela asked.

'Pouring cats and dogs,' Tiffany assured her. 'I ran all the way from the home and still managed to get fairly wet.'

'Ran? Dear me, Nurse Kane—that will never do!' Angela scolded in swift mimicry of Sister Caroline. 'Don't you know by now that a nurse never runs except in cases of emergency—and even that is sometimes frowned on.'

Tiffany laughed. 'Come in, Sister,' she said gaily. 'Angela is just reminding me of one of the first rules of nursing.'

'It's Sister's afternoon off,' Angela said cheerfully. 'You are a wretch, Tiffany.'

'Yes, I know . . . but I couldn't resist it. Has Sister caught you at your clever impersonation yet? It really is clever, you know, Angela . . . when you are well again you'll be able to make a fortune in show business.'

'I hope so . . . it's always been my ambition,' Angela returned happily, knowing perfectly well that she would never be well again, never leave this iron lung until she died, never again walk or run or dance like other girls of her age. She had been a cabaret artiste before polio had attacked her with its unexpected venom—a little dancing, a little singing and a few impressions of famous people had made up her act and while she might not have had star quality she had never been out of work and show business had been her life.

'I'll stand outside the stage door and beg your autograph,' Tiffany promised. 'Preferably on a blank cheque—unless our pay is considerably heightened by that time which seems most unlikely.'

'It isn't very good pay, is it? I know you all complain from time to time—but I always feel that you don't really mind . . . that you enjoy nursing for its own sake and would do the job for half the pay if it was necessary.'

'I suppose some of us feel like that,' Tiffany agreed. 'There must be a lot of truth in what you say, anyway—or a lot of nurses just wouldn't complete their training. I know quite a few girls do leave nursing but it's usually for marriage rather than jobs with better pay. There must be some fatal fascination in nursing, I guess . . . and just one patient like you out of every hundred is more than enough incentive to keep at it,' she added warmly.

Angela coloured slightly. 'Oh, rubbish! I'm nothing out of the ordinary, Tiffany.'

'You're a wonderful person—and I'm proud to know you,' Tiffany replied gently and bent to kiss that flushed face. 'Now I must rush—or I'll have Sister Adeline on my tail.'

She paused to speak to Staff on her way from the ward. 'How is she, Staff?' she asked quietly.

'Not very well just now, Tiffany,' Staff admitted regretfully.

'That's what I thought . . . it's such a waste, isn't it? She's so sweet . . . she had so much to live for . . .' She broke off, biting her lip against a threatened rush of tears.

'Don't get too attached, Tiffany,' Staff said gently. 'I've told you this before. Patients come and go—some of them inevitably die. It isn't good to allow oneself to become emotionally involved . . . I know it sounds hard, unfeeling. I know it isn't always easy to think of patients as case histories rather than as likeable, even lovable people—and of course, one mustn't go quite to that extreme either. It's a question of striking the happy medium. A good nurse doesn't have too much heart or too little heart—compassion in a nurse is necessary . . . emotion that can't help the patient is a waste.' She smiled at Tiffany kindly. 'I'm fond of Angela, too, you know—we all are. But I've accepted that she will die—and I'm thankful for it. I wouldn't want her to spend long, empty, heartbreaking years in a lung—and you shouldn't want that for her either.'

'I don't . . . I just want her to be well again,' Tiffany blurted.

'We all want that . . . we all know that it's just a matter of time before she dies.' She sighed. 'If only she hadn't struggled on with her work in cabaret when she first felt ill . . . if only she could have been diagnosed and treated from those very first few days. But life is full of "if onlys" . . . are you finished or just going on duty, Tiffany?'

'Going on . . . I must run.' She smiled as she turned. 'I daren't, of course . . . I'd be sure to run into Matron at the very least!'

Staff Nurse Hazel Mallory watched her walk briskly from the ward, a faint smile touching her mouth. Thank heavens for Tiffany's irrepressible sense of humour—it would help her to keep a sense of proportion throughout her nursing career. She had been one of the best student nurses they had known on Caroline Ward in years . . . intelligent, industrious, responsible and always cheerful. She had tackled every task with willingness and accepted the most distasteful of jobs with a smile that implied that she knew perfectly well that someone had to do it and if she was that someone then she would get on with it without protest. She had a way with the patients too—a friendly, interested manner that combined concern for their well-being with a determined insistence on their co-operation if they wished to be well again. Tiffany Kane would make a good—an *excellent* nurse . . . *if* she completed her training. That 'if' was inevitably in the minds of her seniors and fellow-nurses for it could not be denied that Tiffany was a honeypot. Without conscious effort on her part, she attracted men—and Hazel Mallory did not think it purely accidental that the first year of her training had been spent on women's wards . . .

Tiffany made her way to her own ward, sublimely unaware that she was known to almost everyone as 'the honeypot'. She was warm-hearted and friendly, treating everyone alike, male or female. To Tiffany, the world was her friend and it never occurred to her to attach particular importance to the attention or interest of men. It was not in her nature to flirt, to set out to attract—and therefore it was unfortunate that a few people had condemned her as an empty-headed flirt in the early days of her training and found no reason since to change that opinion. Tiffany's open friendliness was certainly deceptive to those who did not know her very well. Only the men who had basked in the candid warmth of her smile, exchanged light conversation with her and, knowing an attraction, endeavoured to take matters further could reluctantly admit that there was no thought of coquetry in her approach. For Tiffany had a steady date—one of the medical students—and she had remained faithful to him for over a year, much to the chagrin of those who would like to be able to accuse her of indulging in light affairs with all and sundry.

The first person she met on Adeline Ward was someone who was completely immune to her charm. Staff Nurse Sarah Nelson might grudgingly admit Tiffany's worth as a nurse but she disliked her intensely as a person. All that sweetness and charm was a little too much for the less attractive, less popular staff nurse who condemned the men who smiled and talked to Tiffany Kane as fools, easily deceived by a pretty face and a flirtatious manner. Sarah was much too jealous of the girl to concede that she had a rare loveliness of face and figure and personality . . . in her opinion, the warm affability and smiling good nature was only a façade for a cold and selfish and fickle heart. Sarah prided herself on an efficient impersonality with both patients and nurses . . . she thought that no one could suspect her dislike of the girl, least of all Tiffany herself.

Sarah did not know why she disliked and distrusted this particular nurse so much . . . she just knew that she did and always would and, deep in her heart, she looked forward with some unkind anticipation to the day when everyone else's eyes would be opened to the true character of Tiffany Kane . . .

'Good afternoon, Staff . . . I'm not late, am I?' Tiffany glanced anxiously at the clock—perhaps because her senior had automatically looked at her watch. Quite without realising it, Sarah always hoped that one day Tiffany would break her record for punctuality.

'No, you're not late,' she admitted—and Tiffany wondered if she had imagined the trace of regret. She knew that the staff nurse disliked her—and to Tiffany that was an unconscious challenge. She instinctively turned on her full charm for Sarah—quite unaware that she did so.

'Oh, good! I slipped into Caroline to see Angela for a few minutes—and I might have stayed a bit longer than I intended. Are we busy? What shall I do, Staff?'

'I want you to prepare the trolley for No. 4's dressing, Nurse . . . then you can do the temps and b.p.'s. Don't dawdle for we're short of a junior this afternoon. I shall be in Sister's office if you want me for anything.' With a curt little nod she walked away . . . and Tiffany turned to the routine work of the ward.

Time passed quickly on Adeline which was always a busy ward. It was a women's surgical ward and it was a rare day when they did not have at least one patient on the theatre list. Emergency cases were frequent and kept everyone on their toes and there were always minor ops to be handled . . . patients who had been on the waiting list for admission—hernias, varicose veins, tonsillectomy, dental surgery and others. Patients came and went in rapid succession ... some making so brief a stay that they scarcely made any impression on the nursing staff. Even the majority of patients undergoing major surgery were fit enough to be discharged twelve to fourteen days afterwards, so urgent was the need for beds in this famous and busy London hospital.

Tiffany enjoyed the work immensely. Surgical wards were always interesting ... there was so much to learn, so much continuous activity, so much a feeling of brisk, efficient and generally successful repair to the vulnerable human body. It was rewarding work. One welcomed a new patient, sometimes too ill to know or care what was happening to him: settled him comfortably and strove to reassure his fears; perhaps went with him to theatre and was the first familiar face that he saw when he came round from the anaesthetic; watched and waited during those first hours when life and death might be in the balance; noted the first signs of renewed interest in his surroundings, his fellow-patients, his visitors and his general state of health; observed the daily and sometimes surprising progress and finally wished him farewell with a smile and a friendly warning not to overdo things, watching him leave the ward with a deliberate and often painful briskness in his step which implied that while he believed he was being sent home much too soon, he was glad to go and determined that no one should have second thoughts about his fitness and call him back to his hospital bed.

This was so often the case that Tiffany never

failed to feel a thrill of pride that nursing was her profession. She was always humbled by the skill and dedication of the surgeons who had given these people a new lease of life.

And she was often deeply touched by the often inadequate, awkward, embarrassed thanks of an out-going patient who would all too soon take for granted the miracle that had been worked on his unreliable body, remember only the unpleasant aspects of his sojourn in hospital and devoutly hope that he would never again need to set foot inside St Christopher's . . . the hospital that was affectionately known as Kit's to every member of the staff and not a few of its erstwhile patients.

It was the unsuccessful cases that almost broke Tiffany's self-control . . . she could simply not be as detached as her seniors insisted she must be if she wanted to make a good nurse. There were a percentage of failures, of course . . . there were occasions when a patient who seemed to be progressing well would suffer a relapse and die quite suddenly . . . there were others who underwent surgery even while everyone but the patient realised the impossibility of recovery. There were accident cases who were admitted to a ward only to die within a very short time. There were patients who came in for investigatory surgery only to learn that nothing could be done for them—and it was the sense of frustration that Tiffany and others like her always felt in such cases that made her wonder if she would ever make a good nurse. A good nurse trained herself to accept the inevitable, to look upon patients as little more than case histories who came and went and were soon forgotten, to concentrate her thoughts and energies on doing her work to the best of her ability—and to laugh and talk together lightheartedly even in the midst of death. Tiffany had condemned this last ability as utter callousness when she was a very raw junior . . . experience had taught her that it was a very necessary thing for young and sensitive girls to keep a sense of humour and a sense of proportion about their work.

A death on the ward could still distress her—and it still took some effort to close her mind and heart to what had happened and remind herself that the living required her single-minded attention and devotion.

Tiffany had too much heart. She had not known it would be a disadvantage when she had decided to take up nursing. She loved the job: she wanted to make it her career—but there were times when she wondered if her compassion and affection for humanity would make it very difficult for her to finish her training . . .

CHAPTER TWO

HOWARD Duffy strode into the ward and paused, his keen eyes sweeping over the beds before he met the responsive glance of Sister Adeline who was busy with a patient. He gave her a little nod to indicate his willingness to wait . . . and immediately contradicted that apparent readiness by tapping his foot a little impatiently, albeit unconsciously, while she carried on with her task.

He was a tall, lithe and oddly impressive man with an air of authority that sometimes seemed to border on arrogance. It was said of Howard Duffy that he did not suffer fools gladly: he was reputed to be demanding, autocratic, impatient and intolerant; it was never denied that he was an extremely clever surgeon with an almost complete dedication to his work . . . some said that he would eventually be Professor of Surgery at Kit's . . . others said that his lack of diplomacy in dealing with his seniors and the members of the Hospital Committee would stand in the way of such an achievement.

He was thirty-two years old, recently appointed to the post of Resident Surgical Officer—a latecomer to the field of surgery after first trying his hand at general practice. He was a handsome and eligible bachelor who seemed supremely indifferent to the attractions of marriage and domesticity despite the efforts of various women in his life. His name had been linked from time to time with members of the nursing staff but the rumours soon died a natural death when he displayed an amused contempt for the gossip when it reached his ears.

Howard was not immune to feminine charms—far from it! He liked the company of women but had yet to meet the girl who could stir his emotions to any great or lasting extent. Physical attraction was one thing, he felt . . . the desire to spend the rest of one's life with just one woman was quite another! Surgery was his primary preoccupation in life and he suspected that the woman who would inspire him to a devotion and interest such as he gave to his work simply did not exist. It did not bother him unduly. He enjoyed life: he loved his work; he had many friends of both sexes and his private life was as full and satisfying as he could wish—and deep in his heart he often felt that marriage might be an irksome responsibility for an ambitious man. One would have to be so very sure of marrying the right woman—and how could one ever be sure?

Sister Adeline made her patient comfortable, lingered to reassure the elderly and apprehensive woman and then came forward to greet the young surgeon. He was really very attractive, she thought ruefully, liking him a little too much for complete peace of mind. It was very odd but he was a man who immediately brought a woman's femininity to the fore despite the impersonal starchiness of her uniform.

'Good afternoon, Mr Duffy—what can I do for you?'

He smiled down at her—a tall man, over six foot. It was an endearing smile—one that made warm response completely irresistible . . . a smile that touched his hazel eyes and lingered there long after it had left his lips. Paula Morrow—Sister Adeline for so much of her life that she sometimes wondered if she had lost her real identity—felt her heart lurch a little unexpectedly and instinctively rebuked herself for such folly. She was a ward sister and he was a surgeon . . . he was here purely on hospital business . . . and it was not her business to allow personal and rather foolish feelings to intrude on her usual brisk efficiency.

'Quite a lot, if you will,' he replied courteously. 'I want to talk to you about Mrs Munro's hysterectomy . . . I want to examine the new patient with the valvular irregularity and I want to discuss the list for tomorrow.'

'Then we shall be more comfortable in my sitting-room,' she said briskly. 'Unless you wish to see the heart case first?'

'No . . . we might talk first, I think.' He glanced at his watch. 'You're going off duty at four, aren't you? Your staff nurse can chaperon my examination . . . you won't be very pleased with me if I encroach on your off-duty hours.'

She led the way to her sitting-room, thinking that one of the nicest things about him was his concern for others. Not many of the doctors and surgeons who came to the ward would know or care whether she was supposed to go off duty at a certain time—but Howard Duffy seemed to make it his business to find out whenever he had much to discuss with her. He was considerate and courteous—and those qualities certainly outweighed the faults that were attributed to him, in her opinion.

He was a man who knew his subject thoroughly and wasted no time on preliminaries or hesitation—it was a pleasure to go over any case with him. He was also very good with patients, particularly those who were apprehensive of surgery and that seemed to apply to ninety-five per cent of the cases. The patients claimed that he was kind and friendly and didn't forget to treat them as human beings: that he didn't laugh or shrug off natural fears; that he took the trouble to find out exactly what was on their mind and then explained things in language they could understand; that he was so reassuring and so confident that they felt they could trust themselves to him although he was so young to be a surgeon. Paula sometimes tried to point out that he was not particularly young . . . that some of the surgeons were only in their middle twenties—but she usually had to smilingly agree that he did look younger than his actual age but added that a surgeon was appointed for his ability rather than his years.

She knew just how the patients felt as she sat oppsite him, listening, making notes, answering questions—at times he looked almost boyishly young, particularly when he smiled, but he had a gift for imparting confidence in himself. It seemed unthinkable that he could ever make a mistake where his work was concerned—he took it much too seriously and had studied it much too well. Paula knew that she would place her life in his hands without a qualm—and she was not thinking entirely of surgery.

She wondered with a faint dismay if she was falling in love with this man—a man who had never evinced the slightest personal interest in her and seemed to admire her only as a capable ward sister. It would never do! She knew only too well what havoc it could cause on a ward if a nurse had romance on her mind instead of her work—so many of her juniors seemed to have little else to think about, she thought ruefully. She had worked hard for her position and she was proud of her achievement—and it would need to be a very remarkable man indeed to make her want to give it all up for the humdrum life of a housewife. If only it didn't occur to her all too frequently that Howard Duffy was a very remarkable man . . .

Howard looked up at her quickly, puzzled—and repeated his question. Paula quickly gathered her wandering thoughts and told him what he wanted to know.

He nodded and rose to his feet. 'Well, that's that . . . I'll just have a look at the new patient now and then call it a day. No need to come with me . . . it's just on four, Sister. I'll find Staff or one of the juniors.'

Paula began to tidy her desk. 'I'd like you to manage with a junior, if you don't mind. I must have a word with Staff Nurse before I go off duty.'

'Of course . . . I'll send her along to you,' he assured her. He paused with his hand on the door. 'Are you doing anything exciting with your evening, Sister?' His tone was friendly, casually interested, implying nothing more.

'I expect I shall be putting my feet up and forgetting all about Adeline Ward for a few hours,' she returned lightly. 'The nicest part of being off duty is feeling that I'm Paula Morrow instead of Sister Adeline.'

His smile deepened. 'So I imagine. Do you know, I had no idea that your name was Paula . . . it seems to suit you.'

She wrinkled her slender and rather pretty nose. 'Do you think so? I've always loathed it.'

'Parents will name their children after their own taste, won't they? It would be much more sensible to give them numbers until they are old enough to decide for themselves.'

Paula laughed. 'I think Number Eight must be even more unattractive than Paula!'

He raised a quizzical eyebrow. 'Eight! Good heavens!'

'Oh, I was the last,' she assured him. 'But I agree that it seems an amazingly large family in these days of one or two children. We were as poor as church mice, too . . . but I had a very happy childhood.'

'Of course—why shouldn't you have had?' he retorted swiftly. 'Children are seldom concerned with the material things of life, thank goodness. However, I'm taking up too much of your time,

Sister,' he added briskly. 'And taking too long to get to the point—I have tickets for the new musical at the Unicorn and wonder if you would care to come with me?'

The direct approach took her breath away but she was immediately thrilled by the suggestion. 'I should enjoy that very much,' she said without hesitation.

'Good . . . I'll pick you up at six-thirty and we'll have dinner before the show.' She nodded agreement and he smiled as he turned once more to the door. 'Right—I'm off now or you'll rightly accuse me of making you late for a date.'

As Howard closed the door of the sitting-room and went in search of her staff nurse, he wondered what had prompted him . . . it had certainly not been in his mind until a few minutes before he rose to leave. She was a nice enough girl . . . it was just that she had never attracted him. She did not particularly attract him now—but she was intelligent and rather pretty and he would probably enjoy the evening. It was a much better idea to take Paula Morrow to the theatre than to waste the tickets simply because Shona had decided to be temperamental and break their date. It might be very good for the spoiled and selfish Shona to be reminded that she was not the only pebble on the beach, he thought grimly . . .

Within a matter of moments, he had dismissed both Shona and the ward sister from his mind for the time being. He was much more concerned with allaying the fears of the young housewife and mother who had suddenly developed a cardiac complaint and, because it involved minor surgery, was convinced that she could not survive an operation on her heart. He was scarcely aware of the young second-year nurse who chaperoned for him except to notice that her smile for the patient was reassuring, that she was quick to anticipate his wishes and that there was an unexpected and far from impersonal tenderness in the way that she took the patient's hand and smoothed a tendril of dark hair from the woman's damp and apprehensive face.

But as he rose from the examination and met the nurses's eyes, he was faintly surprised to receive a warm, friendly and completely unprofessional smile. He thought briefly that it was a lovely smile . . . and then he turned back to the patient.

Tiffany was new to the ward and he had been on leave since she was transferred from Caroline so that it was the first time that surgeon and nurse had seen each other. She knew of Howard Duffy, of course—but St Christopher's was a vast hospital and Caroline had been a medical ward so it was not strange that their paths had not crossed.

Tiffany had not thought of him as an attractive man when she smiled across the bed at him . . . she had scarcely thought of him as a man. He was one more member of the human race that she found so fascinating and likeable—it did not occur to her that Sister Adeline might have frowned on such seeming evidence of familiarity between a senior and junior member of the hospital staff. Nurses were not supposed to be anything but automatons, impersonal, brisk, efficient, merely background figures to the doctors and surgeons who surrounded them. It rarely worked out like that, of course . . . but the majority of nurses quickly learned discretion and those who could or would not learn to suppress all human response to the male sex while on duty soon discovered that they were not welcomed in the nursing profession. A certain amount of flirting was carried on—that was inevitable. A considerable number of girls met a future husband on a hospital ward—but the popular conception of hospital romances as conveyed by novels and films and magazines was very much the figment of imagination. Most nurses were kept far too busy to indulge in fanciful daydreams about the male staff and patients: most doctors and surgeons and medical students had other things on their minds but the faces and figures and personalities of the nurses they met during the course of their work.

A student nurse soon discovered that a full social life was a guarantee of failure in her examinations—if she intended to take nursing seriously then she had to limit her pleasures and spend a great deal of time with her books. Medical students might possess the inclination for a series of flirtations but both time and money were lacking.

Howard left the patient's bedside, pleased that he had been able to assure her with truth that she had nothing to worry about, conscious again of that sense of humility which always possessed him when a patient looked at him with complete trust and believed implicitly in his power to heal. He looked down at his hands, strong, masculine with rather short fingers . . . hands that could equally well belong to a manual worker or an office clerk. He thought of the fallacy that a surgeon's hands were always slender and sensitive—and smiled to himself. Nobody cared to believe that strength as well as skill was essential to the hands of a surgeon— surgery was reputed to be delicate work and certainly much of it was delicate and intricate, demanding great concentration and unerring knowledge of what one was doing.

Tiffany straightened the bedclothes, replaced the bed table and returned the patient's chart to its clip. As she turned to leave, she noticed the fountain pen lying on the locker, slightly out of easy reach for Mrs Murray.

'Will you be using your pen, Mrs Murray? Or shall I put it away . . . it might get knocked to the floor by accident.'

Mrs Murray shook her head. 'That isn't my pen, Nurse . . . the doctor must have left it there.'

'Oh . . . I'll see that he gets it,' Tiffany assured her. 'Are you quite comfortable? Can I get you anything?'

'No, I'm fine, thank you, Nurse.' She looked at the clock on the wall above the ward door . . . and sighed. 'It seems an awfully long time to visiting, nurse.'

Tiffany smiled. 'Oh, you'll be surprised how quickly the time will go, Mrs Murray—there's always something happening in a hospital, you know.'

'It seems all meals and doctor's rounds to me!'

Tiffany chuckled. 'Does it? Well, Nurse James is bringing in the medicine trolley now so that's something different. Take your pills like a good girl and try to sleep for a while before supper.'

She caught the surgeon on his way from the ward. He had paused to speak to a post-operative patient and Tiffany noticed how the woman's grateful eyes followed his progress to the door.

'Mr Duffy!'

He turned as she called his name. 'What is it?'

She held out the fountain pen. 'Do you make a habit of littering the wards with your personal possessions?' she asked lightly, teasing him.

Howard frowned, disliking her familiarity for a reason he could not analyse. He had never been a stickler for etiquette . . . and yet it irritated him that this youthful nurse did not seem to have much respect for his position.

'Thank you,' he said coldly, slipping the pen into his breast pocket.

Tiffany was shocked by the hostility of his tone, by the complete lack of response to her warm friendliness. She was so pretty, so natural, so sincere and straightforward in her light-hearted approach to everyone that it was very seldom that she met with a rebuff—and she immediately wondered why he should snub her so unnecessarily. Faint colour leaped into her face. Charitably, typically, she decided that he was a little tired, that he had not realised the abruptness of his manner . . . and so she said warmly. 'You were marvellous with Mrs Murray—she looks a different woman already. She was really terrified, you know—so sure that heart surgery meant certain death.'

'So I gathered,' he returned with that same cool indifference. The compliment meant nothing to him—he decided that she was a pushing little chit who imagined that she had only to smile at any man for him to be bowled over. It was not the first time that he had met with gushing and unnecessary warmth from a virtual stranger—and he had learned to be wary of such people. He disliked flattery even from his friends—he particularly resented and distrusted it from a girl he had never seen before, a girl whose type he recognised only too swiftly, a girl who would boast of her latest conquest if a man merely smiled or looked her way twice.

The snub was unmistakable. Indignation soared in Tiffany's breast . . . what a detestable, arrogant man, she thought swiftly. Too conscious of his position, too conceited and over-confident . . . a good surgeon, maybe, but far from being a likeable or pleasant human being.

He nodded to her curtly and turned away . . . and Tiffany watched him walk down the long corridor, her face flushed and angry. So that was Howard Duffy—well, those who admired him were welcome to him! She had never met such a proud, rude, ill-natured man—and she wished it were possible to tell him exactly what she thought of him!

But he was soon forgotten as Tiffany was caught up in the evening rush of ensuring that everything was in good order for the night staff. Tiffany Kane was not so much in need of anyone's liking or approval that she had to bother her head about a man like Howard Duffy—although she would not have been the genuine, lovable, warm-hearted girl that she was if such a thought had crossed her mind.

And because she found it impossible to bear a grudge or a grievance against anyone, it was inevitable that the next time their paths crossed she should greet him with exactly the same warm friendliness that had originally offended him so unreasonably . . .

CHAPTER THREE

TIFFANY came from the West Country: her home and family were in Somerset, too far for her to make the long and expensive journey to see them whenever she had a weekend off duty. So on these occasions she went to stay with her godmother who lived in Hampstead.

Rebecca Waring was in her late forties and the successful writer of historical romances, a kindly woman with a generous and extravagant nature and a host of friends and acquaintances. Although she had not seen Tiffany since infancy and virtually forgotten her existence she had readily opened her heart and her house to the girl as soon as she learned from one of Grace Kane's rare letters that her god-daughter was training at a famous London teaching hospital.

Tiffany had become very fond of Rebecca—who resolutely refused to allow her to call her 'aunt'— and she enjoyed her weekends in Hampstead. They were so very different to hospital life and although she loved nursing she knew that it was often very necessary to be able to put St Christopher's out of her mind from time to time. That was always possible in Rebecca's company for she had an innate dread of hospitals—for absolutely no valid reason—and never wished to hear about Tiffany's work or studies. The elegance and luxury of the Hampstead house was far removed from the austere efficiency of Kit's and the brisk succession of visitors were usually connected with literature or the theatre or art or music for Rebecca was a renowned figure in London society as a patron of the arts and an indefatigable hostess.

Tiffany was treated like her own daughter—although Rebecca had never married and was quick to scorn the suggestion that she had felt the lack of a husband and children in her successful and busy life. At first, it had been a novel experience for Tiffany to meet so many famous and cultured people but her lack of shyness and her easy, natural friendliness had stood her in good stead and she had usually been accepted without question. If any of Rebecca's friends tended to patronise her or despise her for her ignorance of their way of life, she was blissfully unaware of that fact.

Rebecca's house had become a second home to her: while no one in the world could take the place of the mother she adored, Rebecca came a very good second as a friend and confidante; she missed her family and her home in Somerset but she could be very content with second best when circumstances made it impossible for her to go home.

Rebecca and her mother were remote cousins: their friendship had its roots in the fact that they had been at school together rather than because of the relationship they could claim; they had seen little of each other once Grace married Geoffrey Kane and settled down to domesticity in Somerset but intermittent letters had linked them throughout the years and they had never completely lost touch. Tiffany would never fail to be grateful for that—or for the sentiment that had prompted her mother to ask Rebecca to stand sponsor at Tiffany's christening.

Because she kept what she called her 'party clothes' at Rebecca's, it was only necessary to take nightclothes and toilet things with her for the weekend and Tiffany stuffed them haphazardly into her small case with a stirring of eager anticipation. It was some weeks since she had stayed with Rebecca. Her godmother had been abroad when Tiffany's last weekend came round and a fortnight's holiday at the end of her first year of training had intervened with this weekend. She had visited her for a few hours, of course—but oddly that was never quite the same as staying in the house. One could never forget that St Christopher's was waiting for her time and attention—when she went for the weekend she was able to dismiss everything but a desire to enjoy herself.

It had been a busy day on the ward . . . Fridays always seemed to bring with them an influx of accident cases, either on the roads or in industry. Tiffany had scarcely found time to draw breath so it had been a relief to go off duty, knowing that she was free until Tuesday morning and looking forward to her weekend in Hampstead.

Her room in the Nurses' Home was very small but comfortable. The building had been extensively renovated and modernised at considerable expense and now each girl had a room of her own instead of sharing with two or three of her fellows. Tiffany missed her former room-mates but at the same time she valued her privacy and could appreciate the advantage of being able to study in peace. The room was furnished with the absolute minimum of bed, easy chair and bedside locker but it had a built-in wardrobe and dressing-table cum desk that Tiffany thought both attractive and practical.

She took off the blue and white striped dress with its enormous leg-of-mutton sleeves that could seem extremely plain or amazingly pretty depending on whether or not the style suited the wearer. Tiffany could not make up her mind which category she fell into but she was very proud of her uniform and usually slipped out of it with a vague feeling of reluctance.

But this evening she hurried to change into a dress of soft primrose silk which suited her particular colouring to admiration. It was a warm May evening but nevertheless she decided to take a coat for it could easily be damp and cold by the time she returned on Monday. She took up her handbag and case, gave herself a last glance in the wall mirror, scanned the room hastily to ensure its neatness before Home Sister chanced to inspect it and turned to leave. The door opened abruptly and she stepped back in some haste as Jess Lomax, her friend and fellow-nurse, put her head into the room.

'I hoped I'd catch you,' Jess said thankfully. 'Were you just leaving for Hampstead?'

TREAD SOFTLY, NURSE 35

Tiffany was pleased to see her friend but she hoped that Jess would not delay her too much. She smiled and said lightly: 'No, I'm just about to take a bath!'

'Complete with overnight case? Nothing would surprise me where you're concerned, Tiffany Kane—you're the maddest person I know. Do you realise that Michael is waiting downstairs for you with tickets for the new musical in his hand?'

Tiffany stared at her in dismay. 'Oh no!'

'Oh yes!'

Tiffany clasped her head in mock despair. 'What am I going to do? I'd forgotten all about him, Jess!'

'That's more than obvious!'

'Rebecca's expecting me tonight . . . and she's giving a party that I was particularly looking forward to—Shona Sinclair and Justin Amery are going to be there!'

Jess raised an eyebrow. 'You are hobnobbing with the high and mighties these days, aren't you?'

Tiffany grinned. 'Oh, I know they're only film stars but I did so enjoy *Falling Leaves*—and I can't help feeling that Rebecca has only invited them to please me. You know she isn't particularly enamoured of publicity-seeking celebrities . . . I suppose she fears they might do something outrageous at one of her parties. She might be a little eccentric herself but it's quite unconscious and she never does anything merely to get publicity.'

'I appreciate your dilemma but that doesn't solve the problem of Michael,' Jess pointed out.

'Michael's a dear . . . but . . .' She broke off uncertainly.

'But he can't compete with film stars—is that it?' Jess sighed. 'You *are* mad! Well, he's your boyfriend and it's your big romance not mine . . . but I know which I'd prefer.'

Tiffany wrinkled her brow. 'He may be my boyfriend but it isn't a big romance, as you know quite well.' Suddenly her face cleared. 'I know! Tell him that I've already shaken the dust of Kit's from my heels, sympathise with his disappointment and murmur that it seems a pity to waste the tickets,' she said laughingly. 'You can't fail, Jess—and I know you're just dying to step into my shoes.' She grinned impishly at her friend. 'This is your big moment, ducky . . . make the most of it!'

Jess stared. 'You're not serious?'

'Of course I am! You may have Michael with my blessing—the whole thing is getting a little out of hand anyway. He's very sweet and I like him immensely—but I really don't think I'm capable of *le grand passion* for any man.'

'That's rubbish and you know it. No, Tiffany— I'm sorry but I'm not going to tell lies for you.'

'Even though you'd give your eye tooth to go out with Michael tonight?' Tiffany teased.

Jess coloured. 'Perhaps! But I'm not sure I like the idea of being second best—not even with Michael. Nice of you to hand him over—so noble of you when you just don't want him yourself . . . but I'm afraid Michael wouldn't take kindly to a substitute.'

'You're just being stuffy,' Tiffany objected lightly but she did understand her friend's feelings. It was rather unfortunate that Michael remained obstinately insensitive to Tiffany's lack of real affection for him and so stupidly blind to Jess's prettiness and good qualities. 'Oh, I suppose I'd better see him and explain that I double-dated myself—poor Michael. He *will* be cross with me and try so hard to conceal it.' She sighed—and then straightened her shoulders with an assumed air of going forward to meet danger at all costs.

Jess shook her head in affectionate exasperation. 'You're too kind-hearted, Tiffany—that's your trouble. Instead of brushing him off in the early days when you knew he wasn't quite your romantic ideal you would insist on sparing his feelings and you've been stuck with him ever since—and it isn't fair to Michael, you know. He just gets more deeply involved all the time.'

'He isn't really involved—he just thinks that he is, Jess,' Tiffany said levelly. 'You're right, of course . . . I shall have to break it off before he considers us virtually at the altar!'

The two girls left the room and walked down the corridor to the staircase. They had been close and affectionate friends since the first day of training but, as is often the case, they were poles apart in temperament and character.

Jess was a shy, reticent, rather cynical girl who found it difficult to make friends as a rule and could not approach life with Tiffany's eager capacity for giving wholeheartedly of her liking and interest and affection. She was studious and serious-minded in contrast with Tiffany's natural liveliness and the flippancy which had led her into trouble in the past. She was aware of the darker side of life whereas Tiffany could be astonishingly naive . . . it seemed to Jess that she was for ever warning her friend against the dangers of offering friendship to all and sundry but it certainly appeared that Tiffany had a guardian angel perched on her shoulders for she was generally liked and respected and favoured a little more than was really good for her. Jess feared that one day she would suffer a severe setback and, while she considered that Tiffany needed to grow up a little in some ways, she did not want her to mature abruptly through disappointment and humiliation.

This ridiculous affair with Michael Gilroy was typical of Tiffany. Everyone but Michael himself seemed to know that she thought of him as nothing more than a friend—and she simply could not bring herself to disillusion him. For over a year she had been dating him and although he was not her only date it was becoming widely supposed that she preferred him to any other man. But that was certainly far from the truth—and Tiffany was foolish to have allowed matters to drift to the point where a great many people were half-expecting their engagement to be announced. Tiffany simply would not believe that this was so—and if anyone questioned her on her 'romance' with Michael she automatically assumed it to be a joke and replied in similar vein instead of taking steps to kill the rumours. Jess did her best but it was not pleasant to realise that she was suspected of wanting Michael for herself. Perhaps she was a little in love with him, she admitted courageously—but her sole concern was for his feelings when he eventually did learn the truth. She had no hope that he would turn to her for consolation—he had never shown the slightest interest in her except as Tiffany's friend!

He was waiting patiently in the hall and turned as he heard their steps. He came forward eagerly with a confident smile for Tiffany... a smile that faded as he saw the case she carried and recognised its implications.

Tiffany rushed into speech. 'Oh, Mike... I *am* sorry to be such an idiot! When we made plans for this evening I'd completely forgotten that it's the beginning of my weekend off! I wish I could come with you but Rebecca will have made such plans for tonight—and I haven't the heart to disappoint her! I know *you* understand, though—but you really should be furious with me!'

'That's impossible,' he said, a little stiffly. 'I'm sorry, too, Tiff... I managed to get tickets for *The Golden Girl*—you did say you were longing to see it.'

'And so I am! It's so annoying—but there's really nothing I can do but go to Rebecca's... you see, I promised her faithfully I'd spend the entire weekend with her—and that was before we made arrangements for tonight. I don't know how I could forget it was my weekend... because I was so rushed just then, I suppose.'

'It can't be helped,' he said quietly. 'I'll drive you to Hampstead instead.'

'Oh no!' She almost shrieked the words, knowing that she would not be able to avoid inviting him into the house and knowing too that good-natured Rebecca would insist that he stayed for the party—and he would loathe every minute of it. Michael was not the party type . . . he had once accompanied her to one of Rebecca's parties and it was a mistake that Tiffany did not mean to make a second time. 'You mustn't waste the tickets! I know you must have been all over town to get them—and it will ruin my entire weekend if you don't see the show after so much effort! Jess will keep you company,' she added unblushingly, not daring to look towards her friend who would certainly throw her a glance to slay her on the spot. 'You don't mind, do you, Jess?' And now she did look at the girl whose mouth had tightened with visible annoyance. 'It wouldn't be very kind of you to make Michael go on his own, after all—and I'm determined that the tickets must be used!'

'I expect Michael has plenty of friends . . . it won't be difficult for him to find someone to go with him,' Jess retorted.

'Well . . . if you'd *like* to go, Jess,' he said uncertainly.

'No . . . really, thanks. I don't care for musicals,' she assured him, ignoring Tiffany's stifled gasp of horror at the bare-faced lie.

'Pity . . . well, never mind—I expect Noel will leap at the opportunity,' Michael said awkwardly.

'Of course he will,' Tiffany assured him confidently. 'Get in touch with him . . . you must hurry for you haven't much time if you want to get into your seats before the show starts.'

She almost pushed him from the Nurses' Home—and he was so embarrassed by the little incident with Jess that he was not reluctant to make his escape.

'Honestly, Tiffany . . .!' Jess exclaimed indignantly. 'You'll go to any lengths, won't you—except do the decent thing and let him down gently.'

'It wouldn't be a gentle let-down after all this time, however I tried,' she retorted. 'But honestly, Jess . . . !' she mimicked teasingly. 'How could you turn down such an opportunity?'

'Because I'm not going to be bull-dozed by you—and I won't allow Michael to be forced into something so obviously distasteful to him.'

'Oh, you're much too sensitive!' Tiffany told her gaily.

'And Michael was so persuasive, wasn't he?' Jess retorted with faint bitterness.

'He was just surprised by the suggestion, that's all,' Tiffany said reassuringly. 'I wish you'd taken it up, Jess—I'm sure you're kindred spirits if only you'd give yourselves a chance to find it out.'

Jess laughed involuntarily despite her natural indignation and humiliation. It was impossible to be cross with Tiffany no matter how justified one's annoyance—she had such a simple, appealing faith that her friends had only to take her advice for their lives to run as smoothly and as satisfactorily as they could wish. As though an evening with Michael brought about by Tiffany's tactless and blatant matchmaking could possibly prove to be the beginning of a wonderful friendship!

'You're absolutely hopeless!' she declared with mock exasperation. 'When will you learn that you can't push Michael and I into each other's arms when it's the last thing on earth that either of us want?'

Tiffany gave her a long and searching glance. Then she said quietly: 'That isn't strictly true—but let it pass. I'm afraid I handled things badly . . . if I'd had more time you and Michael would have been happily setting off for the theatre quite unaware that I'd engineered it.'

Jess raised an incredulous eyebrow. '*I* could never be unaware of your intentions at any time, Theophanie Kane!'

Tiffany groaned. 'Oh hush! You never know who might be listening . . . I'm going before you dredge up any more of my dark secrets!'

And she went with a swish of silk and a rapid staccato of high heels, leaving Jess to make her way slowly up to her room and the text-books that were waiting for her attention . . .

CHAPTER FOUR

THEOPHANIE!

Tiffany groaned again as she sat on the cool leather seat of the taxi that was taking her across London. She had never been able to understand how her parents could have brought themselves to saddle her with such an outlandish name—and they must have regretted it for she had never been anything but Tiffany since she was a baby, thanks to a lisping, three year old brother.

She could live with *Tiffany* although few people accepted it without question as her name . . . *Theophanie* was something she preferred to forget. But most of all she loathed *Tiff*—and could not break Michael of the tendency to use the absurd abbreviation.

Michael was a nice, thoughtful and considerate young man—but he was getting to be such a bore, she thought ruefully. He was steady, level-headed, reliable and predictable . . . Tiffany knew the way his mind worked, how he reacted to most situations, what he would do and say well in advance.

She was fond of him in a sisterly kind of way but her emotions were as untouched as though he had always been the 'boy next door.' She was very sure that Michael felt exactly the same way about her. She knew perfectly well why they had dated each other so regularly since the earliest days of her training. Tiffany had a very practical streak and she had decided that while she did not want to dispense with male company and attentions entirely, as had some of her fellow students, she had no desire or intention to become romantically involved with any man—and Michael could certainly not afford to date any girl who cherished thoughts of love and marriage while he was only a medical student and as he was not a sensual or romantic man by nature he did not find it difficult to keep his emotions under control.

Michael was the ideal boy-friend in such circumstances—there had never been any talk of romance between them and nothing more than the occasional casual, almost meaningless kiss or embrace. Tiffany knew from occasional remarks he had let fall that he vaguely assumed that they would eventually drift into an engagement and thus into marriage at some distant date. Tiffany knew that this would never happen . . . she was already too much of a habit in Michael's life and she did not mean to marry any man who was content to drift so carelessly with the tide. *If* she ever married at all—and that was entirely dependent on whether or not she met a man she could love and who would love her in return—then it would be a marriage based on mutual love and need and the knowledge that life would be empty and pointless apart. She could never feel this for Michael—and he would never feel it for her.

But their easy, undemanding relationship had

suited them both admirably . . . Tiffany had been spared the advances of the wolves who imagined that no woman could be happy without their attentions and Michael had been able to concentrate on his studies to the full.

Lately, she had begun to realise that this idyllic relationship could not continue. Lately, she had begun to sense that Michael was taking her for granted—and she had also begun to wonder if he imagined that she was in love with him. He had been taking her out for over a year and perhaps he did not fully realise the platonic nature of her feelings. Perhaps he thought that she had a right after all this time to expect him to care for her and to want to marry her. He was not the type to play fast and loose with a girl's affections . . . he *was* the type to attach real importance to the rumours that linked their names. Perhaps it seemed to Michael that she believed herself virtually engaged to him— and nothing would induce him to let her down if that was true.

Tiffany frowned. If he did chance to be thinking along such lines then she would have to make a break with him. It would not do, she thought resolutely. She would miss him to a certain extent but it might not be a bad thing if she gave more time to her studies now that she was in her second and more demanding year of training. Even the two evenings a week that she spent with Michael might be more profitably spent with her textbooks. Or she could accept an occasional invitation from other men if she wished to avoid any hint of emotional entanglement as so many of her colleagues managed to do.

She would break with him anyway, she decided abruptly. For all she knew, it was possible that he was getting more involved than he could wish at this stage in his studies . . . she very much doubted it, knowing Michael so well, but one never really knew and she did not want to risk hurting him at some later date. He was fond of her, she knew . . . he might even imagine himself in love with her—the taxi drew into the kerb and with a start of surprise Tiffany realised that she was at her destination. She stepped out to the pavement, paid off the taxi and pushed open the white gates. As she walked towards the house she knew the familiar feeling of excited anticipation and a warm sense of homecoming.

Rebecca was relaxing over a pre-dinner cocktail, glancing idly through a sheaf of magazines and mentally checking her guest list and the arrangements for the party. She had an excellent secretary who could be trusted to ensure that nothing was overlooked but Rebecca liked to organise her parties herself down to the last detail. She was looking forward to the evening with pleasure—it was truly said that no one enjoyed Rebecca's parties as much as Rebecca herself and perhaps that was the reason for their success. Her own enjoyment was infectious and she spared no pains to ensure the enjoyment of her guests.

Tiffany paid a brief visit to the room that was always kept in readiness for her to leave her case with the well-trained maid who would not only unpack for her but also lay out the dress she had chosen to wear that evening. Then she hurried to announce her arrival to her godmother.

Rebecca tossed the magazines aside as Tiffany entered. She held out her hand to the girl with a warm, radiant smile. 'There you are! Aren't you a little late?' There was curiosity rather than reproach in her tone.

Tiffany stooped to kiss the smooth cheek that Rebecca proffered. 'A slight contretemps with the boy-friend,' she explained gaily. 'Then I couldn't get a taxi—and, to crown it all, we seemed to catch every traffic light and traffic jam in the whole of London. Are you dying for your dinner, Rebecca? I'm so sorry!'

Rebecca brushed the apology aside. 'Just ring the bell, will you, darling . . . Jeeves will know that I mean him to serve dinner.' Her butler had the prosaic and, to Rebecca, much too common-place name of Smith—she had re-christened him Jeeves as a joke and now neither Rebecca nor her many friends ever called him anything else. No one knew what Jeeves thought of his new name . . . he had always answered to it with perfect aplomb. 'Pour yourself a cocktail if you want one.' Rebecca stubbed her cigarette and removed the stub carefully from the long gold holder that she affected. Many of her little eccentricities were carefully affected— or had been in the early days of her success as a writer and had now become so ingrained that not even Rebecca knew which was affectation and which were perfectly natural to her. If anyone remonstrated with her, Rebecca invariably pointed out that everyone expected a writer or an artist or a musician to be dramatically different from the rest of mankind and she did not have the heart to disappoint them.

They were not disappointed for Rebecca Waring was a flamboyant and striking personality. A stout woman, she would not play down her size but emphasised it in the face of all opposition from her dressmakers: she adored jewellery and wore masses of it on all occasions, disregarding convention by looping diamonds about her neck, wearing rubies on her wrists and emeralds in her ears and an assortment of precious stones on her fingers; ignoring the advice of her hairdresser, she insisted on having her platinum-blonde hair piled high on her head and she horrified her maid by being as lavish with cosmetics as she was with her jewels. For some unknown reason, the combination did not dismay her friends and acquaintances. She *should* have looked ostentatious and ridiculous and rather common—but if she did no one ever noticed. Her appearance was outweighed by the warm sincerity and true pleasure of her greeting, the radiant, bewitching smile, the husky warmth of her rich voice and the generous humanity and interest and delight in her fellow-beings that emanated from the stout, over-dressed, over-adorned figure of London society . . .

Tiffany refused the cocktail. Staying with Rebecca and mingling with her sophisticated friends had not encouraged her to adopt their habits. She did not like alcohol and she could not smoke a cigarette without gasping and choking like an idiot. So she wisely steered clear of both . . . and did not make the mistake of condemning others for their addiction to either.

'That's a new dress, surely, Rebecca?' she said, knowing that her godmother loved her to take an interest in her appearance.

Rebecca beamed. 'You *did* notice! *How* I depend on you, darling! I knew that you would remark on it if no one else did. Do you like it?'

As it was a particularly uncomfortable shade of electric blue, Tiffany could not honestly say that she liked it. So she said in all sincerity: 'It's *you*—there's no doubt about it. No one else could wear it so successfully.'

'I expect I look hideous but you're much too kind a child to say so . . . I *do* look hideous but there isn't much point in a woman of my size trying to look elegant, is there? If you can't win compliments then for heaven's sake draw comments—that's my motto and always has been! Ah, there's the gong.' She heaved herself to her feet. 'I haven't ordered a heavy meal, of course—we'll be having a buffet later. But I think I've chosen some of your favourite dishes, Tiffany.'

Tiffany did not doubt it. That was one of the nice things about Rebecca . . . she took the trouble to find out what one liked and supplied it when she could.

They did not linger over the meal. Tiffany had to

change and Rebecca expected guests to join her for coffee. Their arrival happened to coincide with Tiffany's movement towards the stairs but she paused only to greet them with a smile and a few words, knowing them well.

Such sophistication! she teased herself as she changed for the second time that evening. It was at such times that she felt like a lady of leisure—and found it easy to forget all about the hospital. And that could be a good thing for a young girl who seemed to eat, breathe and sleep nursing for most of her daily life.

Rebecca was much too good to her, she thought happily as she stepped into the simple green dress that her godmother had insisted on providing for these occasions. Tiffany felt the velvet dress was an extravagance but she could not really feel guilty about accepting the gift from someone who was not only her godmother but also one of those people who found pleasure in showering gifts on those she loved.

She hastily tidied her hair, deciding to leave it in the neat, practical roll that suited her small face and gave her confidence and then it was the work of a moment to renew her lipstick. She wore little make-up and felt herself fortunate to have a good skin and a natural, healthy colour although she deplored the freckles which she could never disguise. They were a mere smattering on her nose that few people noticed but to Tiffany at times they were an unsightly disfigurement. She was not a vain girl but those freckles did bother her occasionally.

Rebecca looked up in surprise as Tiffany entered the room where she sat with her friends. It was always a source of amazement to her that a young girl could get dressed for a party in so short a time . . . she needed the entire day in which to prepare before she was satisfied with her face and hair, her clothes and her jewels. But she had to admit that no amount of lengthy preparation could better Tiffany's appearance. She was a very presentable young woman with the glow of youth and health and anticipation in eyes and cheeks and parted lips: the dress was a perfect foil for her colouring, and she never made the mistake of altering the simplicity of the hairstyle which suited her so well or trying to adopt the sophistication which simply was *not* Tiffany by plastering too much make-up over her sweet and lovely face, thought the woman whose taste in such matters was notoriously execrable. Rebecca *knew* what was correct—she just did not choose to conform. But that did not meant that she was ignorant of what was right for other people— and she thought that Tiffany had never looked more 'right' than she did this evening.

She noted with satisfaction that it was not only her opinion as Giles Cavendish automatically gravitated to Tiffany's side. His father, engaged in conversation with Rebecca, was too well-mannered to follow suit but Rebecca rather fancied that he envied his son. She was proud of Tiffany whom she regarded rather in the light of a protégée. She had been dubious when she first introduced the girl into her particular aegis of society but she had soon realised that Tiffany was much too sensible and level-headed to be spoiled by her immediate success and popularity. She knew exactly how much or how little importance to attach to the extravagant compliments and particular attentions which came her way: she did not encourage any man unduly and, to Rebecca's knowledge, had never met anyone socially except in her house; she was liked just as much by the women as the men except for one or two obvious exceptions and it never seemed to occur to Tiffany that people were friendly for any other reason but that she was friendly towards them.

She was not a girl without a heart: indeed, Rebecca often thought that Tiffany had too much heart. But while her friendship and her affection were bestowed generously she did not flirt or encourage men to flirt with her and no one who knew Tiffany could imagine that she would either want or enjoy a long string of conquests to her credit. She would not fall in love easily, Rebecca thought shrewdly, but when she fell it would be heavily and for the first and last time and one could only hope that the man she chose to love was both suitable and responsive and, most of all, appreciative of his good fortune.

'Rebecca, my darling, I know I'm a prosy old bore but you might at least make the pretence of being interested in my remarks,' Paul Cavendish chided her lightly.

Rebecca was immediately contrite for Paul was one of her oldest and dearest friends and in dwelling on thoughts of Tiffany, she had broken one of her strictest rules. She hastened to atone, to apologise and to assure him that she was interested but her thoughts had wandered for the merest moment.

He had followed the direction of her thoughtful gaze and now he said quietly: 'Not worrying about Giles, I hope? His intentions are quite honourable, I believe.'

Rebecca chuckled. 'I really don't think it would make the slightest difference if they weren't, Paul! Tiffany is such an innocent—I doubt if it ever occurs to her that a man might have sex in mind when he pays court to her!'

'She's a woman, my dear,' he said pointedly. 'I know enough about women to know that they are always very much aware of what is going on in a man's mind!' He glanced at Tiffany and his son with smiling indulgence, noting the complete lack of coquetry in her manner as she looked up at Giles with a warm smile and responded to some remark he had made. 'She's a charming child,' he went on, patting Rebecca's hand. 'But not quite to my son's taste, you know—that's why you have nothing to worry about.'

'I never worry about Tiffany,' she retorted promptly. 'She's very capable of taking care of herself—and I believe that her obvious innocence will protect her from all but the worst type of man. And I certainly don't encourage those people to my house so Tiffany is safe enough with anyone she meets here.'

That remark prompted Paul to discuss the guest

list for the evening and they were deep in comfortable, slightly gossipy conversation when they were interrupted by the arrival of some of those guests...

Tiffany was enjoying herself. She liked Giles Cavendish, overlooking his slightly bohemian tendencies and knowing that his conversation or his manner would never disturb her no matter how rakish he might seem with other women later in the evening. She knew Giles well by this time, knew that he tended to drink a little too much, knew that he was something of a womaniser but he was always courteous and kind to her and she had never yet found cause to complain of his behaviour where she was concerned.

Tiffany could never understand why some girls displayed pique and indignation when a man failed to respond to an obvious approach... for her part, she was never flattered or pleased if a man evinced more than friendly interest. She was not a prude—she simply respected herself and expected others to respect her equally as much. She could only give her kisses to a man who inspired her affection... casual, meaningless kisses left her completely cold and with an instinctive desire to extricate herself from the man's embrace. She was certainly not cold-blooded... it was merely that she did not want a long line of casual affairs to her credit when she met the one man she could love—if such a man existed!

She sipped her fruit juice and listened while Giles talked about his work, quite content to provide an ear for the rather egotistical young man who found his father's fame as a sculptor a challenge to his own dream of equal fame as an artist in oils. She always refused to sit for him, believing his request to be flattery rather than real desire to capture her image on canvas—and, try as he might, he could never persuade her to change her mind.

He was trying once more when the new arrivals came into the room—and Tiffany was so preoccupied with reiterating her reasons for refusing that she did not notice their entrance.

They were followed by others and suddenly the large room seemed full of people, all talking at once—and the party was abruptly in full swing . . .

CHAPTER FIVE

REBECCA moved among her guests with greetings and exclamations of delight and pleasure, smiling and talking and radiating warmth and vitality and hospitality.

She came to the celebrities she had invited partly to please Tiffany, partly because they were the current rage of London's society and it must never be said that Rebecca Waring ignored the claims of any one of society's darlings to experience the delights of one of her parties.

At first sight she had heartily disliked the beautiful Shona Sinclair who had entered the room with an air of gracious condescension. Second sight did not improve her opinion of the spoiled, sophisticated young woman who kept a possessive hand on an arm of each of her male companions and seemed to be sharing her favours equally between them. Rebecca thought cynically that the girl was determined to be noticed . . . her voice was a little too pitched to carry, her smiles were a little too dazzlingly artificial—and her dress was low-cut almost to the point of indecency. Rebecca did not deny that she was beautiful in a sultry, exotic style with her raven hair caught up in a cluster of curls high on her head and her dark, rather bold eyes gleaming in a lovely, camellia-like face. But she was not a type that Rebecca liked or approved . . . she was a man-eater, she thought grimly and wondered, not for the first time, that men could be such fools as to fall into the clutches of such a woman without the slightest attempt to save themselves.

Justin Amery, the girl's co-star in the very successful film, was already known to Rebecca for they had met at a luncheon party given by a mutual friend. Rebecca liked him: he was a modest, unaffected man who could not conceal his surprise at having touched the heights of stardom almost overnight after years of hard work as an actor; success had not gone to his head . . . he had every expectation of finding himself once more appealing to his agent for work within a very short time, convinced that this sudden stardom was no more than a flash in the pan. He was no longer young, happily married to a woman unconnected with the theatre who was quite content to stay at home with their children while he was temporarily lionised by society, and although rumour and gossip had already linked his name with that of Shona Sinclair, Rebecca did not think there was any fear that the Amerys would find themselves in the divorce court.

The other man was a stranger to Rebecca, a remarkably handsome man who had failed to recommend himself to her for anything but his looks because he had unsuccessfully disguised his amused incredulity at her appearance when she first sailed across the room to greet them.

Now she paused to carry out her duties as hostess, to ensure that they were supplied with drinks and cigarettes, to make any introductions that might seem necessary at such an informal gathering to thank them warmly for attending her party and to hope that they would enjoy the evening.

'Such a delightful room!' declared Shona with the air of bestowing the final accolade. 'I adore the decor . . . surely I recognise Winston Clark's touch?' She mentioned the name of a well-known specialist in the field of interior decor.

Rebecca grinned. 'All my own work—and Winston deplores it every time he comes. If you admire his art, don't tell him that you thought this room was his creation when he arrives—he'll be your enemy for life!'

Faint annoyance touched the lovely girl's expression and Rebecca was pleased to have scored a hit. But she was quick to recover her smile. 'Oh, will *he* be here tonight?' Shona asked, her tone implying that Winston Clark's arrival would absolve this party from winning the prize as the most boring and commonplace she had yet attended.

'Well, I am expecting him—but Winston is always late,' Rebecca said lightly. 'He likes to avoid those who only drop in for a drink en route to other parties—and quite a few do, you know.' She knew she had scored again as Shona looked vaguely discomfited and glanced instinctively towards the unknown man by her side. He was looking at Rebecca, a faint smile lurking in his eyes—and she glanced at him with the merest lift of an eyebrow that questioned his right to enjoy himself at her expense when she did not even know his name.

He recognised that faint hauteur and his smile deepened. 'I don't suppose you caught my name, Miss Waring,' he said levelly. 'It's Howard Duffy . . .'

'My fiancé, you know,' Shona broke in carelessly.

'I didn't know . . . I'm sorry, Mr Duffy. I'm delighted to welcome you to my home.' She held out her hand to him, smiling.

'Thank you.' His clasp was firm and confident. 'It's a lovely home if I may compliment you on it,' he went on. 'I believe it has been featured in a magazine . . . I didn't see the photographs but I'm sure they couldn't have done justice to the reality.'

Rebecca beamed at him. She lavished loving care and great expense on her home and her taste was faultless where the house and its furnishings and decor were concerned. Nothing pleased her more than to be complimented on its beauty and elegance. He could not have said anything more calculated to endear himself to her . . . and she was immediately confident that it had not been calculated at all. He did not strike her as a man who would waste his time with idle flattery. He really did admire her house and had not hesitated to say so . . . and from that moment he was assured of a place in her intimate circle of friends even if she deplored his taste in women.

'How nice of you to say, Howard . . . I may call you Howard, I hope?'

'Of course.' He inclined his head briefly.

'You must come to see me again when the house isn't so full of people,' Rebecca urged warmly. 'I bore all my friends with extolling the virtues of the place—but I can provide you with an excellent meal to allay your boredom!'

Howard laughed. 'I'll take you up on that invitation,' he said lightly. 'And not only for the promised delights for my inner man. I really am interested in houses and the Georgian architecture is almost an obsession with me.'

'Then we'll arrange a date before you leave tonight,' Rebecca assured him. 'Now . . . if you'll excuse me, I must circulate—Justin, come with me . . . I want you to meet the Cavendishes, father and son. Paul is the sculptor, you know—and Giles is carving a place for himself as a portrait painter.' She chuckled. But her amusement was not only for the deliberate play on words that she had voiced but also for the chagrin which leaped to Shona Sinclair's face as Rebecca neatly annexed her co-star and left her with only one man on which to feed her vanity.

Rebecca thought that it would not be long before she was surrounded by men—she did not attach much importance to the engagement that apparently existed between Shona and Howard Duffy. The girl wore no ring and there was nothing of the possessive lover in his manner. No doubt Shona was the type of woman who announced every man in her life as 'her fiancé' in order to score off other women who were as yet unattached.

Justin excused himself with a smile and went with Rebecca, carving a passage through the crowded room with his broad shoulders. He looked down at Rebecca with faint reproach in his glance. 'You don't like poor Shona,' he said and it was not a question.

Rebecca snorted inelegantly. 'Poor Shona!'

'Oh, she's very misjudged,' he said grinning. 'She's just a simple girl at heart with a natural yearning for domesticity.'

'I pity the poor devil who falls into her trap,' Rebecca said bluntly. 'I've never seen anyone less suited to domesticity. There's talk about you and Shona Sinclair, Justin.'

He nodded. 'I know.' He was quite unruffled.

Rebecca linked her hand in his arm. 'I never pay much heed to gossip,' she assured him. 'People will say anything! It's obvious to me that you haven't much affection for that affected little madam!' She touched Tiffany's shoulder and the girl turned towards them. 'You wanted to meet Justin Amery, my dear,' she said lightly. 'Well, I promised I'd bring it about . . . Justin, this is my god-daughter, Tiffany Kane.'

Tiffany lifted a laughing face. 'Isn't Rebecca tactless!' she exclaimed. 'Now I feel like one of those silly schoolgirls who hound you for your autograph!'

Justin smiled. 'You don't look in the least like an autograph-hunter or a schoolgirl, I assure you—no book, no pen and, regretfully, not the slightest hint of awe and adulation.'

'Oh, I'm sorry! I've ruined the party for you!' she exclaimed lightly.

'You have indeed, Miss Kane—I'm used to stepping over every woman I meet, you know, and you haven't shown the least inclination to fall at my feet in a swoon of delight.'

'It must be a terrible bore for you,' she said swiftly, sincerely.

'Oh, yes . . . but one does come to expect it,' he replied, smiling.

'Let me get you a drink instead?' she offered.

'A most acceptable alternative,' he agreed. 'But I won't allow you to wait on me . . . what are you drinking, Miss Kane?'

She gave him her empty glass. 'Fruit juice, please . . . and my name is Tiffany.'

Rebecca, whose attention had been claimed by another of her guests, turned back to them. 'I think I can leave you quite happily, my dears. Tiffany will look after you, Justin . . . I promised to introduce him to the Cavendishes, darling—do it for me, would you?' She slipped into the crowd.

Justin smiled at Tiffany. 'I don't really feel that I would have much in common with the Cavendishes, father and son, you know,' he said lightly. 'I'd much rather talk to you . . . you're going to hate me for saying this but you remind me very much of my daughter. She has the same mischievous sense of humour and complete lack of respect for my fame.'

Tiffany chuckled. 'How old is she?' she asked with that swift, warm interest in other people that always endeared her to them.

'Three years old,' he said. 'May I bore you with details?'

'Please do!'

'I'll supply you with a drink first . . . I find that most people need some form of sustenance when I'm talking about my family.'

Tiffany looked after him, smiling, liking him as she instinctively liked so many people and liking him particularly because he did not try to conceal the fact that he was a proud father at a party where he might be expected to forget everything but the company, pleasing or otherwise, of the girl to whom he had been introduced.

He had scarcely returned to her side when Howard Duffy came up to him and spoke his name. Justin turned to him politely. 'You look a little lost, old man—what's happened to Shona?'

'Otherwise engaged,' he said drily, indicating the group that almost concealed the slender figure of the dark-haired girl. As he turned back he looked full at Tiffany for the first time . . . and she stared back at him in ill-concealed astonishment, having immediately recognised the arrogant young surgeon.

'I know you, don't I?' he asked abruptly, frowning, trying to recall where they had met but unable to place her face—and vaguely irritated by her evident surprise.

'We've met,' she agreed, the corner of her mouth twitching with amusement. She wondered how long it would take him to recognise her out of the uniform that, some people claimed, made every nurse look alike. In Tiffany's experience, few strangers bothered to look beyond the uniform at the girl who wore it—and she was not surprised that Howard Duffy should have failed to recognise her.

'I meet a great many people,' he retorted, annoyed that she obviously expected him to play guessing games, knowing an immediate antagonism towards this young girl with her air of serene self-possession.

'This is Tiffany Kane, Howard,' Justin broke in, coming to his rescue. 'Miss Waring's god-daughter, I understand.'

The name meant nothing to him. Again he frowned. But he managed to instil a little courtesy into his abrupt: 'How do you do?'

Tiffany was seized with the childish impulse to snub him, to humiliate him—unpleasant man! Then all her charitable instincts rushed to the fore, erasing her indignation. It was not fair to tease him, she thought penitently. He was a busy man . . . one could not expect him either to know her name or to distinguish one nurse from another when he was hurrying about his work on the wards.

'I'm in my second year at Kit's,' she told him lightly. 'We met on Adeline the other day—remember? I returned your fountain pen.'

'Oh . . . yes, of course.' He was little more than necessarily polite, remembering also that this was the girl who had deliberately thrust herself to his notice, the girl whose obvious coquetry he had chillingly snubbed, the girl he had successfully dismissed from his mind a moment after leaving the ward.

Justin was puzzled by the awareness of hostility between them. He had known that Duffy was a surgeon: he had only now learned that Tiffany was a nurse; from his experience, members of the same profession usually fell on each other's necks with delight. But he realised that Duffy was antagonistic to a natural and friendly young girl who had a great deal of charm and an attractive personality—he seemed to resent her presence at this party! Was it a question of hospital etiquette which had always seemed to Justin so unnecessarily harsh and impersonal? Duffy did not impress him as a man who would stand on his position—but at the moment he was certainly far from pleased at meeting socially a nurse from the hospital where he worked.

Justin only knew of Tiffany what he had sensed or learned for himself . . . she might be a femme fatale, anathema to the male staff at St Christopher's—and perhaps Duffy was wise to be wary of becoming socially acquainted with the girl. But this was a chance meeting—it had not been engineered by anyone and Duffy should have the courtesy to respond to Tiffany's warm friendliness without making it obvious to everyone that he found it a cause for mistrust!

'Can I get you a drink, Howard?' he asked lightly, striving to ease matters.

'No, thanks . . . I must go back to Shona before it becomes impossible to reach her side.'

Tiffany spoke impulsively: 'You must mean Shona Sinclair! Do you know her well? I admire her talent so much . . . she's very beautiful, isn't she? But now that I've seen her in the flesh, I'm rather disappointed—she seems such a cold, proud person . . . not in the least as I'd imagined! Am I wrong? Is it a false impression?'

She was taken aback by the shaft of sudden anger in his hazel eyes. 'I don't know how she may seem to you, Miss Kane,' he said coldly. 'But you can scarcely expect me to share that view . . . Miss Sinclair and I are engaged to be married.'

Tiffany could not conceal her instinctive surprise. There was little about the private lives of the senior staff at Kit's that was not public knowledge and there had been no doubt in anyone's minds that Howard Duffy was not a marrying man.

Howard interpreted that flicker of expression as dismay and thought grimly that he had taken the wind out of her sails if she had imagined that this party would be an excellent opportunity to become better acquainted with him! It had never been his policy to associate with junior nurses other than in the course of his work but he frequently found it necessary to discourage a girl who believed she could alter his views. It was so obvious that Tiffany Kane—and the name was as ridiculous as her ambition!—was as insufferably conceited as all the others. It was unfortunate that they had chanced to meet at this party that Shona had insisted he should attend . . . it was equally unfortunate that he had been prompted by a swift mounting of dislike to claim that Shona was his fiancée. He was not engaged to Shona: he was not yet sure that he even wished to be—and he had only been stayed by a reluctance to humiliate Shona when she had introduced him as the man she was going to marry. The announcement would be all over London by the morning—and, thanks to Tiffany Kane, all over the hospital!

But it might do no harm if he was believed to be engaged to Shona Sinclair . . . he was growing weary of avoiding and snubbing determined young women. At times, he was bewildered by the whole thing—one would imagine him to be the only unattached man at Kit's! He had never thought himself particularly attractive to women but there seemed to be some strange alchemy in the atmosphere of a hospital—and some nurses could not resist flirting with any man in a white coat.

Howard was not much interested in casual flirtations on or off duty nor particularly anxious to be married—not even to Shona whose beauty and capricious moods and exotic personality had held him captive long after he might have tired of another woman. He was not in love with Shona but she was exciting and desirable and she chose to keep him guessing as to her real feelings for him. Whether by accident or design, this provocative behaviour sustained his interest—and their affair had been in progress long before she attained stardom.

Tiffany had coloured to the roots of her hair at the realisation of her *faux pas*. 'I'm so sorry,' she said ruefully. He looked at her with swift, suspicious enquiry in his eyes and she realised that again she had said the wrong thing. 'I mean . . . I wish you every happiness, of course,' she hastily added. 'If I'd known, I wouldn't have been so free with my opinion . . . I mean—I'm sure she isn't really proud or cold . . .' She trailed off as she glanced at Justin and saw the effort he was making to suppress his laughter—she was very tempted to laugh herself but she knew that Howard Duffy could not appreciate the amusement of the situation.

'As it happens, your opinion doesn't carry any weight in the matter,' Howard said coldly. 'And I don't know that I'd be particularly impressed with your ability to judge a complete stranger, if it did.'

'I've offended you . . . really, I'm sorry,' Tiffany said warmly, her innate wish to befriend even the rudest of her fellow beings coming once more to the fore.

He shrugged. Without even bothering to reply, he turned to Justin and began to talk to him, excluding Tiffany from the conversation and his notice . . .

CHAPTER SIX

WITH a murmur of excuse, Howard left them . . . and Tiffany looked at Justin with a faint bewilderment in her eyes. But he had no explanation to offer for the unexpected discourtesy of a man who was usually so pleasant and affable.

He said easily: 'I guess you two just don't like each other.'

Tiffany gave an expressive little shrug. 'We don't really know each other,' she replied carelessly. 'Surgeons and nurses are not encouraged to mix socially, you know . . . I'm a very junior nurse—the lowest of the low to an RSO.' Justin looked blank and she laughed involuntarily. 'Resident Surgical Officer,' she told him. 'Quite a plum post for a young man—and he isn't much more than thirty, is he?'

'I really don't know, Tiffany . . . I've only met him once or twice in Shona's company when there hasn't been much opportunity for exchanging confidences. Shona believes a conversation is pointless unless it's centred on her, you know.'

Tiffany glanced at him with mock reproach dancing in her eyes. 'I guess you two just don't like each other,' she said, echoing his own words.

'No,' he admitted. 'Despite the gossip, Shona

and I are only seen together on unavoidable occasions.'

'Is there gossip?' she asked quickly. 'I haven't heard any, Justin.'

'You will,' he assured her grimly.

'But if Shona Sinclair is engaged to Mr Duffy . . .' she began, puzzled.

'If,' he echoed with a faint smile.

'Isn't she?'

'Shona likes to be engaged to the man of the moment regardless of whether or not he's got around to proposing,' Justin told her bluntly.

'But Mr Duffy . . .'

'Was backing her up for reasons of his own. To the best of my knowledge, Tiffany—and I think I would know—there's no official engagement in existence. Shona would leap at the opportunity for publicity and I imagine she'd over-ride even a man like Duffy who might be expected to want an engagement kept dark for the time being.'

Tiffany wrinkled her forehead in perplexity. 'But what reason could he possibly have for emphasising to me that he's engaged to her?'

It was his turn to move his broad shoulders in a shrug. 'That, my dear, is something you should know for yourself. I haven't any idea at all. But I agree that he certainly intends you to believe that he's engaged to be married.' His eyes twinkled. 'Have you been trying to lure the poor man into a compromising situation, young woman?'

'I haven't the slightest inclination to do so!' she retorted with faint indignation. 'I think he's a rude, arrogant man—and Shona Sinclair is welcome to him, for my part! Do you know, he almost wiped the floor with me the other day—and all I did was to return his wretched fountain pen,' she said heatedly. 'I wish I'd snubbed him as mercilessly when he came up to us, Justin—it would be very good for him to have some of his conceit knocked out of him!'

'Steady on!' Justin remonstrated, grinning. 'You'll set the place on fire with those blazing eyes. You really have got it in for each other, haven't you—it must be a case of Dr Fell!'

'I don't know . . . it seems to be where he's concerned but on the two occasions that I've spoken to him, he's given me very good cause to detest him,' Tiffany replied. 'I wish I knew why . . . it just isn't reasonable. Oh, well . . . let's not talk about him any more. You were going to tell me about your family,' she reminded him.

He was quite willing to change the subject—and, as he knew no one but his hostess, Shona and Howard Duffy at this party, he was content to spend his time talking to this sweet and likeable young girl who showed no inclination to desert him for a younger or more eligible companion . . .

Tiffany was grateful to him. She could have circulated among the guests and never lacked for company or conversation . . . but Justin Amery was so pleasant, so easy to talk to and so interesting that she did not want to be drawn away by others or to interrupt the beginnings of a welcome friendship. She gladly accepted an invitation to his house in Surrey one weekend, to meet his wife and children—and knew that she would look forward to the visit. He was kind without patronage, genuinely interested in her as a person and, she sensed, completely trustworthy and much too devoted to his wife to mean anything but friendliness by his interest.

She was grateful because Howard Duffy's odd and unreasonable hostility had ruined all her enjoyment of the evening. She had no heart for the gaiety and high spirits of the evening and knew that her vivacity and gaiety would only be forced if she were to mingle with the other guests. It was more pleasant to talk quietly with Justin Amery and to watch other people enjoying themselves on this particular evening.

She had been hurt by the surgeon's obvious dislike of her and by a certain annoyance in his manner that she should have been a fellow-guest at this party. Did he imagine that a mere student nurse had no right to attend a party together with some of London's more famous celebrities, she wondered indignantly. Or was it merely that he liked to forget Kit's when off duty, as she did—and had resented the reminder of his professional life on an occasion connected with his private affairs? Either reason did not explain why he should have thrown his engagement at her head in that fashion! It had been as blatant as a 'Keep Off' notice! Surely she had not done or said anything to give him cause to suspect that she was attracted to him! If he thought that, then he was as colossally conceited as she had suspected—and all because she had approached him on Adeline Ward with a friendly smile and a quip! No . . . it was much too ridiculous to suppose such a thing.

She knew that there were some girls who would go to any lengths to attract the interest and attention of the handsome RSO—but she had done no more than return his pen to him! Surely he did not believe she had used the opportunity to try to attract him . . . why on earth *should* he think such a thing? If she had been one of the hospital flirts she could understand his wariness . . . but it was so much more than wariness. He had been distinctly antagonistic, full of dislike and hostility . . . he had looked at her with definite loathing and hurried away rather than be forced to exchange further conversation with her. And not just on one occasion . . . but twice!

Once more, she promised herself hotly—and she would demand an explanation. RSO or not, she was entitled to courtesy from him! Not that she would go out of her way to come in contact with him . . . and if her work on the ward forced a meeting then he would discover that she could be as cold and punishing with her expressions and tone as himself!

Tiffany was seldom aroused to anger—and as she had a hot and impulsive temper, it was perhaps as well that she was usually quick to make allowances. Incurring a person's dislike was not new to her although it did not often happen and naturally she did not expect to be universally loved . . . she did not always try to find out the cause for the dislike and eradicate the first bad impression. But when dislike was accompanied by arrant bad manners, particularly in public, then her temper flared and pride outweighed her tolerant good nature . . .

Howard tried to dismiss the girl and concentrate on the vivacious, lovely Shona and give himself to full enjoyment of the evening. But for most of the evening, Tiffany Kane was in full view as she talked and laughed and danced with Justin Amery. Whichever way he turned, she seemed to move within his range of vision . . . and it was impossible to close his eyes to her presence in the large and crowded room.

He seethed with annoyance each time he caught sight of her . . . and looked away with deliberate coldness if their eyes chanced to meet. He meant to leave her in absolutely no doubt of his indifference to her presence.

He did not pause to analyse his unreasonable dislike of Tiffany Kane. It was enough that he had disliked her intensely from that very first meeting on Adeline Ward . . . and distrusted her motives in hurrying after him and quizzing him so familiarly. He despised her type . . . and as he watched her playing up to a man quite old enough to be her father, coquettish in her pretty pretence of admiration and interest, he was filled with angry contempt. She was old enough to know better, he thought irrationally . . . having just condemned her as too young and irresponsible and conceited to realise that she was making a public spectacle of herself and inviting gossip by a deliberate play for the mature and attractive actor.

He would not have minded so much if he had been in the least deceived by her simulated interest in Justin Amery. But her eyes would keep straying to where he stood with Shona and he was conscious that her glance followed him about the room . . . once, when their eyes chanced to meet, he looked away coldly but not before he had observed a swift surge of guilty colour to her face.

The silly chit! Did she, like those others, think she had only to smile and he would be at her feet? Well, she would not get any encouragement from him . . . he had put her firmly in her place twice and that should be enough for any ambitious girl. And yet she still tried to draw his attention . . . once even smiled at him across the room—and he suspected that she would use this accidental social encounter to full advantage if she was given the merest opportunity to do so.

It was all so ridiculous . . . a man grew tired of brushing off the advances of girls who had nothing better to do, it seemed, than try to inveigle him into a meaningless flirtation. There was not a girl at Kit's who could hold a candle to Shona—and even if there had been, it would never do to allow his professional and personal interests to overlap. He had made that mistake once—and his work had suffered for months. That had happened during his student days and it was an incident in his life that was almost forgotten . . . perhaps because he had no wish to remember the pain and humiliation of that affair.

It was years ago now . . . and since that time, he had avoided the snares that many women had laid for him. Until he met Shona, no woman had been able to excite his interest more than briefly.

Shona might be spoiled and selfish and a little too conscious of her attraction for men but she had intelligence and personality as well as beauty. She was also inclined to be too possessive, too confident of her hold over him, too demanding and jealous of his love for his work—and perhaps she had become little more than a habit in his life. But if he ever gave any thought to marriage at all it was usually Shona that he visualised as his wife—but he could never make up his mind if it was affection or the desire for a lovely, sophisticated and socially acceptable woman who could help him in his career that prompted the image. He would certainly never think of marrying a girl like Tiffany Kane. Oh, he did not deny that she had a certain appeal . . . the glow of youth and health, a *joie de vivre* and a marked prettiness—another man might leap at the opportunity of her favours. But her particular brand of charm left Howard unmoved—and it was not doing her vanity any good to have Justin Amery dancing attendance on her, he thought irritably as the sound of their easy, intimate laughter reached him.

'You're positively glowering, darling,' Shona murmured, linking her hand in his arm as she turned briefly from the attentions of another man 'Dare I hope that you might be jealous?'

'Of your popularity—not in the least,' he replied promptly. 'I merely admire his taste which coincides so well with my own. I suit you much too well to be easily replaced, Shona.'

She chuckled. 'That arrogance! It will lead you into trouble one day, Howard.'

'Not for the first time, I assure you!'

'Why were you scowling? Aren't you enjoying it? Shall we go?' She smiled up at him. 'You aren't chained to me, you know, darling . . . if you want to seek other company for a while, I don't mind at all.'

He raised an eyebrow. 'You're singing a different tune to the usual one, Shona . . . perhaps I do have cause to be jealous of that overgrown puppy?' She did not reply immediately and he turned to look at her. 'Well?'

Her glance was faintly coquettish. 'Giles is a very sweet boy,' she said lightly. 'But, between ourselves, I prefer my men to be a little more mature.'

'Then go and talk to Justin and extricate him from that designing little chit,' he said before he could check the words.

Shona looked at him in surprise. 'I've never known you to sound so vicious, Howard . . . what has the poor girl done to you?' She glanced across at Tiffany with some curiosity. 'Who is she, anyway?'

'Rebecca Waring's god-daughter or some such

thing,' he said impatiently. 'Justin has scarcely left her side all evening.'

'So? He seems to be happy enough—and I've never known Justin to put up with being bored or cornered when he didn't choose to be,' she said lightly. Her eyes narrowed. 'Do you know her, Howard—I mean, did you meet her before tonight?'

'She's a nurse,' he said briefly.

'From St Christopher's? Oh . . .' Her hand tightened abruptly on his arm. '*I* wouldn't have cause to be jealous, by any chance, darling?' she asked, lightly enough but with the hint of swift anger behind the words.

'Good God, no!' he exclaimed, revolted. 'I know her by sight—that's all.'

'Then why so vehement?' she pressed sweetly.

'Drop it, Shona,' he said curtly, annoyed with her and with himself for a stupid sensitivity where the subject of Tiffany Kane was concerned.

Her eyes hardened but she had no opportunity to flare at him as Giles Cavendish appeared at her side with the drink he had gone to get for her. She pointedly withdrew her hand from Howard's arm and turned a cool shoulder to him as she welcomed Giles with unnecessary warmth.

Howard moved away from them, ostensibly to speak to Justin as he passed with empty glasses, making for the bar. The two men exchanged the briefest of remarks before Justin continued on his way . . . but in that momentary break Shona and Giles had been joined by others and Howard found himself on the outside of the vivacious group and completely indifferent to the fact.

He made his way through the crowd to the open windows that led out to the stone terrace, the thought of clear, cool air suddenly appealing to him. He decided to smoke a cigarette in peace and privacy. It was a dark night, the moon hiding behind clouds and only the distant stars and the light from the house behind him relieving the warm, sultry deep of the night.

He leaned on the stone balustrade beside a pillar, the scent of roses rising from the garden below, the faintly discernible sound of traffic from the distant road murmuring in his ears when the sound of music and laughter and the babble of voices stilled abruptly. He turned to realise that someone had closed the windows but the person who crossed the terrace towards him had her face in shadow and only the gleam of her hair prompted him to guess that it was the last person in the world he wanted to talk to in a terrace tête-á-tête.

He stepped forward, crushing his cigarette underfoot, with the intention of returning immediately to the house . . . and Tiffany almost jumped out of her skin.

Her exclamation of surprise was well-feigned, he thought cynically. 'Did I startle you?' he said coldly. 'I'm sorry.'

She looked up at his austere, arrogant face in the muted light from the windows. 'Oh, it's you,' she said and her tone was far from friendly. 'I didn't think anyone was out here . . . I didn't mean to disturb you.'

'You haven't . . . I'd finished my cigarette and was about to return to my fiancée,' he assured her coolly.

It was so obvious that he could not bear to exchange even the merest pleasantries with her that Tiffany was perversely prompted to detain him. 'I hope you're enjoying the party,' she said lightly. 'It seems to be a great success.'

'Naturally you must think so,' he said smoothly but contemptuously. 'After all, you've made a very flattering conquest—even if Amery is almost old enough to be your father.'

Heat of sudden anger seared her face. How dared he! He was the most insufferable, nasty-minded man she had ever known! How dared he sneer at the warm and innocent friendship which had leaped to life between her and Justin? How dared he smear that friendship with vile implications? Impulsively she raised a hand to slap his face . . . but she could not follow out that impulse. There was something in the mocking challenge of his eyes that hinted that it was exactly what he would expect of a young, foolish girl who had not yet learned to control her temper.

She tilted her chin defiantly. 'Isn't it said that the onlooker sees most of the game?' she asked with deceptive carelessness. 'It hadn't occurred to me that Justin was particularly smitten—but if that's so then I am having a successful evening indeed. I think he's quite the nicest and most interesting man I've met to date.'

If he chose to believe that she had deliberately set out to captivate Justin Amery then why should she deny it . . . why should she have to explain or defend herself to an arrogant and ill-mannered man she scarcely knew? It was none of his business what she did—and she was tempted to tell him so, having found it intolerable to feel his watchful gaze on her throughout the entire evening.

'You obviously don't realise the dangers of casting out lures to a married man—a happily married man, at that,' he said with deliberate patronisation. 'Justin is whiling away a dull evening with the flattering company of a silly young girl with stars in her eyes whenever she looks at him. But he'll forget you the minute he leaves this party—and you'll be wise to forget him, too. Take some advice from someone older and wiser than yourself . . . avoid throwing yourself at a man's head—it's always a mistake!'

Tiffany stared at him speechlessly—and before she could find her voice to flay him mercilessly for his insolent presumption, he turned on his heel and left her.

In that moment, for the first time in her life, Tiffany knew exactly what it meant to loathe someone with an intensity that startled her . . .

CHAPTER SEVEN

THE sun streamed through the open windows of Adeline Ward, shafting its bright, bold, merciless rays across the beds and their occupants. Those patients who were not allowed up but had recovered sufficiently to complain when things did not suit them, tossed and turned restlessly, could not settle to any occupation and grumbled incessantly about the heat.

The end of May had brought a heat-wave that was much too intense and unexpected for the average Briton. On this particular morning there was not a vestige of a breeze to make the warm weather a little more bearable and Tiffany, flushed and perspiring, her red hair damply clinging to her scalp and the starch of her apron swiftly disappearing as she hurried and scurried about her work, could sympathise with the grumblers. Even the cooling system seemed powerless to combat the still, suffocating, glaring heat that was so enervating and caused tempers to shorten so rapidly.

The ward was quiet in comparison with its usual hustle and bustle. Unless an emergency case came in, there were no patients to be prepared or taken to theatre for it was Sunday: the post-operative cases were following the anticipated pattern and only one patient in a side ward was giving anxiety;

several patients were being discharged that day and there would not be a new intake until the following morning. It was Sister Adeline's weekend off and Staff Nurse Nelson was in charge of the ward. The nurses on duty, assigned to routine tasks, grumbled cheerfully about the weather and the dull work and looked forward eagerly to going off duty and the chance to change from uniform into cool, sleeveless dresses more suitable for the weather.

Sarah Nelson disliked being in charge. She was not afraid of the responsibility and the junior nurses knew better than to dispute her authority at any time. It was the amount of paper work which irritated and depressed her . . . she did not like sitting behind a desk, dealing with forms and certificates and case histories. She enjoyed working with the patients, taking a more active part in the running of the ward—administration was not really her metier and it was on occasions such as this, when Sister was off duty and she had to take over, that she knew that the achievement of her 'strings' would be an empty victory although she had worked for them since the earliest days of her nursing career.

Soon, she expected to be offered her own ward for Sister Philadelphia was due for retirement—and she would have to make up her mind whether to accept or refuse. It was doubtful if she would be able to remain at Kit's if she refused for it was training hospital and only a percentage of qualified nurses were offered posts—the others were expected to find employment elsewhere. A staff nurse who was chosen to train for a sister's position but who decided to refuse the responsibility would be expected to make way for a more ambitious girl.

Sarah knew that she was a good nurse—but she was too modest to believe herself indispensable to Kit's. If she refused the offer of a ward then she would have to look about for a position in another hospital. She would be reluctant to leave Kit's—but at times she felt equally reluctant to become a sister. She had thought about private nursing but decided it would not suit her after the demanding, arduous but always enthralling work on hospital wards. Nor was she attracted to the idea of a provincial hospital after so many years of working at a busy London hospital with its many specialised departments.

She had turned the problem over and over in her mind, and still did not know the answer. But on this particular morning, hot, weary and bored, she rather thought that a sister's strings would not suit her at all.

She was a nurse not a clerk, she thought crossly as she drew yet another discharge certificate towards her and began to fill it in ready for signature. How thankful these patients must feel to be going home, well again but for the period of convalescence before them—Sarah knew that no amount of gratitude in a patient's heart for the care and skilled attention he or she had received at St Christopher's could ever outweigh the relief and thankfulness of discharge. Few patients liked being in hospital no matter how much was done to ensure their comfort and well-being—and it was almost hurtful to realise how swiftly they left the hospital precincts, how soon they would be grumbling about an imagined lack of interest and attention, how rapidly they would cease to be grateful for all that had been done for them. But not really hurtful for, after all, surgeons and doctors and nurses knew that this was a healthy and welcome reaction—and no nation wanted or could handle a race of hypochondriacs. The fear and dislike of hospitalisation was an excellent thing although it might sometimes seem unreasonable and unjustified.

Sarah filled in the last of the discharge certificates and collated them with a faint sigh. All they needed now was the signature of the RSO or one of his housemen.

She glanced up at a nurse who passed, pushing the trolley laden with the empty trays of those patients who were not allowed to join the up-patients in the dining-room at the end of the ward. She looked at her watch and verified its accuracy with the electric clock above her head. She was due to go to lunch—and she was quite relieved to do so for Sundays were too quiet for Sarah unless they were enlivened by emergency cases and she liked them even less when she happened to be in charge of the ward.

She checked over the nurses on duty in her mind . . . it seemed that Nurse Kane, a mere second-year, was the most senior of the juniors on the ward at the moment—and Sarah frowned. Nurse Wells had been granted extra leave because her mother was ill and Nurse Murray had been taken to the sick bay the previous evening with appendicitis. Because Sunday was usually so quiet, Sarah had decided that she could manage the ward without applying to Matron for replacements—and she would only be away from the ward for an hour. Nurse Kane should certainly be able to cope and it was not as though she would be entirely alone on the ward. Sarah reminded herself that personal dislike should not affect her knowledge of a nurse's ability or sense of responsibility—she had no reason to suspect that Tiffany Kane lacked either of these things. She was willing and conscientious and good-natured—and she had to gain experience of being in charge of a ward eventually.

But when Sarah finally went to have her lunch, having primed Tiffany well and added as many cautions as she could in a few minutes, she still felt vaguely uneasy—if only it had not been Tiffany Kane even though she might seem a good nurse. Things seemed to happen to that young woman—there was no denying it. Sarah could cite a dozen instances that had been cause for hospital gossip and amusement—the most outstanding, perhaps, the unforgettable incident on Prudence . . .

Tiffany's first experience of ward work: very nervous, very raw and very gullible. Prudence was a woman's medical . . . the patient in question had come in for investigation with a history of abdominal pains, backache, low blood pressure and sudden weight increase. She had been on the waiting list for admission for several weeks and had been admitted to Prudence the day before Tiffany Kane was sent to the ward to work. Pausing in her assigned task of tidying the lockers, she had enjoyed a conversation with Mrs Phillips which sent her scurrying to Sister Prudence who had smiled tolerantly down at the junior who suggested that the patient should be moved to a maternity ward immediately. Patiently, Sister Prudence had pointed out that neither the woman's own doctor nor those who had examined and questioned her at the hospital had found any reason to suspect pregnancy—and the woman herself insisted that it was out of the question. Tiffany Kane had listened with demure attention but seemed quite unconvinced—and even while Sister Prudence was talking there was an anguished cry from the patient they discussed—and within moments she was being hustled to the labour ward where she gave birth to lusty, full term twins within the hour.

Sister Prudence had never quite forgiven her new junior who had no reasonable or acceptable explanation to offer for her conviction that Mrs Phillips was expecting a happy event . . . all she would say was that she recognised a certain look in the woman's eyes and while that might have been accepted from an elderly matron it was impudence from a girl scarcely out of her teens. No one at Kit's could feel that 'a certain look' in a woman's eyes was evidence of pregnancy when experienced and qualified doctors had failed to detect any other signs . . . and everyone felt that Mrs Phillips and the new junior had conspired together in an attempt to make fools of the medical profession. Such cases were not unknown but they were rare . . . and the doctors concerned with Mrs Phillips could comfort themselves only with the reminder that she was by nature a big woman and this, combined with her indignation and immediate rebuttal of the suggestion that she might be pregnant, had led them to consider other causes of her symptoms and complaints. She had been admitted for investigation . . . if her twins had not chosen to be born so untimely they would have discovered the truth very shortly—and it was mere chance that a junior nurse had paused to talk to Mrs Phillips just as she went into her short-lived labour.

It was probably rather unfortunate for Tiffany Kane but since that incident every ward sister who came into contact with her had eyed her rather warily—and Sarah Nelson was not the only person who felt that things happened to this particular nurse that would not happen to other junior nurses. It was no fault of her own . . . it was just one of those things.

So Sarah went off to have lunch with a vague disquiet—and Tiffany, quite ignorant of her senior's unflattering thoughts, carried on with her work in the heat of the day without the least expectation of being called upon to discharge any duties as the nurse in charge . . .

She was reassuring an anxious relative over the telephone when the swing doors of the ward were pushed open and Howard Duffy strode in. Tiffany's heart sank. He would choose this particular time to visit the ward, she thought resentfully—and wondered if he would concern himself only with the patient he had probably come to see or if he would want to talk to her at all.

He paused by the desk and looked about him, obviously in search for someone in authority. Tiffany finished her telephone conversation and replaced the receiver. 'Good afternoon, Mr Duffy,' she said with all the icy hauteur she could muster.

He nodded . . . a brief, curt nod. 'Where is Sister Adeline?'

'She isn't on duty today, I'm afraid.' So you'll have to exchange conversation with me, like it or not, she added silently.

'Staff nurse?' He was deliberately abrupt. He did not mean to get involved in idle conversation with this forward little chit.

'At lunch.' Tiffany was equally as abrupt—and she noticed the flicker of annoyance that touched his eyes. The arrogance of the man! He could bark out his questions with impunity—but no one must dare to return his rudeness!

'Then who is in charge of the ward?' he asked—or rather demanded with some impatience.

'I am. What can I do for you, Mr Duffy?' She smiled with deceptive sweetness.

His eyebrow quirked abruptly. 'It isn't customary to allow an inexperienced junior to take charge!' he said cuttingly.

'We happen to be short-staffed today,' she told him, keeping her temper with an effort. 'Staff Nurse will be back in forty minutes.'

He glanced at his watch. 'I can't spare that much time—and I won't be on duty for the rest of the day.' His tone implied that it was entirely her fault that there was no one more responsible to attend to him.

'Then you'll have to put up with me, won't you,' she said quietly, drily.

His eyes narrowed. 'Don't be impertinent to me, girl—or you'll find yourself reporting to Matron!' he snapped.

'I don't think I have to tolerate that tone from you or anyone else, Mr Duffy,' she flared, keeping her voice low. 'Please state your business and leave my ward!'

He stared at her incredulously . . . and then he laughed, softly, mockingly. '*Your* ward, Nurse?'

'For the time being—yes! If you care to take the point to Matron I'm perfectly willing . . . and I'm sure she will uphold me,' Tiffany told him calmly.

He continued to look at her . . . and now his smile was reluctantly becoming warmer, faintly admiring. The impudent little devil . . . taking that tone to him and telling him to leave *her* ward! Brief authority had evidently gone to that ridiculously red head! But despite his natural resentment at being addressed so peremptorily by a second-year nurse and his instinctive dislike of this girl which nothing could ever alter, he felt a sneaking admiration for her spirit—and he knew that she was right to a certain extent. He had been unnecessarily rude to her: after all, it was nothing to him who happened to be in charge of a ward when he entered it—he had only come to Adeline to sign discharge certificates and a junior nurse could attend to that formality with him; she was temporarily in charge and therefore vested with all the authority of a sister until someone more senior relieved her of the responsibility and both custom and etiquette dictated that she should receive all the respect and courtesy due to a sister.

'I don't think that will be necessary,' he told her. 'I'm sorry . . . I shouldn't have allowed personal feelings to intrude. I believe you have some discharge certificates that require my signature?'

'They're here,' she said and picked them up to hand them to him.

Their hands brushed briefly as he took the certificates—and the contact was annoying to them both. He glanced through the completed forms, took out his fountain pen and began to append his signature to each one. Tiffany watched him coldly, anger still hot within her breast—and mingled with that anger was a queer, disturbing pain. So he had allowed his personal feelings to intrude, had he? Exactly what did that explanation mean? Did he detest her so much that the mere sight of her could banish his brisk, formal manner and easy courtesy and stir him to harsh, insulting rudeness? How could she possibly have offended him so deeply? Was it merely a case of ineradicable and inexplicable dislike on his part? She disliked him thoroughly—but not without cause. He had never been anything but rude and aggressive and hostile towards her—and one could not like a person who so obviously resented even being in the same room as one! Tiffany had never been so conscious of dislike and hostility in anyone before—and it had never hurt her so much as this man's unreasonable and unfair antagonism. Surely she was entitled to know why he disliked her so much? Surely she was entitled to know why he felt that she did not merit courtesy from him let alone his respect? She had heard of natural antipathy between two people but Tiffany could scarcely believe that such a thing could exist between virtual strangers without good cause—and she had searched her memory in vain to find a reason for his animosity. Not that it could possibly matter to her—she had no desire for his liking or his good opinion . . . and it was absolutely ridiculous to allow herself to feel vaguely hurt by his manner.

Howard sensed her intent gaze and he looked up with a hint of enquiry. Tiffany looked away coldly, realising that she had been staring down at his proud, dark head as he bent over the desk and concerning herself far too much with a man she did not even like. There was no need to even think about him except when their paths crossed on the ward . . .

He signed the last of the certificates and pushed them across the desk towards her. 'Do you want me for anything else? Were there any messages from Nurse Nelson?'

'I don't think she expected you to visit the ward today, sir,' Tiffany told him.

'Probably not . . . anyway, I'm just going off

duty. For the rest of the day—Mr Savage will be on call.' He nodded to her with cold formality and turned on his heel.

Tiffany gathered up the discharge certificates and went to distribute them to the anxiously waiting patients, most of whom were dressed and ready to leave the hospital. She was able to dismiss Howard Duffy from her mind as she became involved in bidding farewell to the outgoing patients . . . but during the rest of her time on the ward the thought of him kept recurring to irritate and disturb her usual serenity.

She was sure that it was not merely an over-active sense of etiquette that kept him so cold and indifferent and formal. She had seen him in smiling conversation with junior nurses . . . seen how he stiffened and broke off the conversation when she approached. It was obvious to her fellow-nurses that he had no time for Tiffany and she had borne many a curious glance and airily dismissed many a probing question as to the evident hostility between them. She did not expect the RSO to behave with undue friendliness towards any junior nurse—that would soon give rise to gossip. But he seemed to be bending over backwards to impress upon everyone that one junior nurse in particular was his *bête noire*—and Tiffany resented the interest that his behaviour was arousing in her colleagues.

She did not intend to put up with much more of it: she had already promised herself a reckoning day with Howard Duffy—and it was not far distant. All she needed was the right opportunity to accuse him of singling her out for a marked display of dislike and bad manners—and to demand an explanation. An opportunity would never present itself on the ward unless she wished to create a scene before the patients—and she had no way of knowing if and when they would meet in different circumstances. If necessary she would go to Matron to complain of his behaviour—and while that would not ease his dislike it might be the means of putting an end to his public rudeness.

CHAPTER EIGHT

HOWARD turned a corner and almost collided with Sarah Nelson . . . he instinctively clasped her arm to assure himself that she had kept her feet.

Sarah laughed up at him. 'I didn't know you could be so impetuous, Mr Duffy . . . you were almost running!' He smiled and murmured an apology and she went on with a faint note of disappointment in her voice: 'You've just left Adeline, I gather?'

'Yes . . . the discharge certificates are signed. There wasn't anything else you wanted to talk to me about, I suppose?'

Sarah shook her head. 'Everything seems to be under control . . . or at least it was when I left,' she added wryly. 'I didn't feel too happy about leaving Nurse Kane in charge, I'm afraid.'

He raised an eyebrow. 'Isn't she a good nurse?'

'Oh, very promising—but she is only in her second year and emergencies have been known to arise when juniors are left to cope alone.'

'Well, I can relieve your mind—the ward seems very quiet and peaceful,' he assured her.

'Then I really needn't have hurried over my lunch,' she said ruefully. 'I missed coffee—but if I'm not needed on the ward just yet I'll make myself a cup, I think.'

'I'll join you, if I may,' he suggested.

Sarah was faintly flattered. She had never been particularly impressed by the looks and the charm of the man who seemed to set so many hearts fluttering and certainly he had never gone out of his way to be anything but courteous and impersonal where she was concerned. This sudden desire for her company was a new development and she was too much of a woman not to think complacently that she was about to score over many of her colleagues who would give their eye-teeth for a little private conversation with the RSO.

'Of course,' she said lightly . . . and they walked along the corridor to Sister Adeline's sitting-room, talking idly of the heat wave, the improbability of it lasting much longer and whether or not it boded a good or bad summer . . .

Sarah prided herself on being able to make an excellent cup of coffee and she knew she had not failed on this occasion as he sipped it appreciatively and glanced up to commend her skill with a smile and a nod. 'Just the way I like it,' he told her—and Sarah pigeonholed the information for future occasions.

She sat opposite him in a comfortable armchair, her slender legs elegantly crossed. Howard brought out his cigarette case and snapped it open. Sarah hesitated for only a moment. 'Well, I'm not officially on duty yet,' she said serenely and took a cigarette from the case. He produced his lighter and flicked it into flame.

'It's nice to relax for a few minutes, isn't it?' he

mused, leaning back in his deep chair. 'I don't suppose you enjoy taking over from Sister Adeline.'

'Oh, I don't know . . . there are certain aspects of being in charge that do appeal to me,' she replied with a faintly coquettish smile. 'Sister keeps everyone very much on their toes, you know . . . I'm afraid I shall never be so much of a martinet. And, without blowing my own trumpet too much, I do seem to get an equivalent amount of work out of the juniors by my laxer methods. I don't believe in hounding them—unless they are obviously lazy or slapdash, of course. Sister tends to exhaust herself chasing them about the ward.'

'I imagine you get on well with the juniors,' he complimented vaguely.

'Oh, I think so,' she agreed complacently. 'For the most part . . . I do have some difficulty with Nurse Kane, though,' she admitted, a little spitefully. She had not been impervious to his open dislike of the girl and she had been faintly pleased that someone else should share her feelings where Tiffany Kane was concerned. She could not resist this seeming opportunity for a little back-biting.

'Any particular reason?' he asked without much interest but realising that her excellent coffee demanded its own price.

Sarah shrugged. 'Oh, I don't know . . . a kind of dumb insolence, I think. Do you know what I mean? She hasn't very much respect for anyone in authority, it seems to me—some people believe it's just natural friendliness but I'm afraid I don't care for undue familiarity from a junior nurse. I don't stand too much on ceremony, of course, but I do like the patients to be aware that I'm in charge and not just another junior nurse,' she ended a little crossly.

'I think I know what you mean,' he said, not wishing to be drawn into criticism of a nurse.

'Oh, I'm sure you do, Mr Duffy,' she said impulsively. 'Why, I've seen her treat you like an orderly or a porter at times—and I don't blame you in the least for putting her in her place. People like Tiffany Kane need it occasionally. Another thing,' she went on, warming to her subject. 'She simply cannot resist flirting with any man who comes on to the ward—and it doesn't matter a scrap whether he's a student or the Professor himself! I suppose she must have a certain attraction for men—but I'd have imagined that most men dislike a girl who throws herself at their heads.'

'Some men are reluctant to snub that type of woman,' he told her carelessly, a little anxious now to finish his coffee and make his escape. He was vaguely contemptuous of her obvious spite.

'It seems to me that a great many of them encourage her,' Sarah retorted tartly. 'Really, her behaviour on and off duty is common gossip . . . no one would imagine that she was engaged to be married and I'm only surprised that any man will put up with her ridiculous flirtations.'

Howard's attention was caught despite his complete indifference to the girl in question. 'Engaged, is she? Well, perhaps she means no harm by her flirtations,' he said with an effort at charity. 'Her fiancé probably understands that it is nothing but ordinary friendliness.'

Sarah almost snorted. 'He must be completely besotted,' she said unkindly.

Howard set aside his empty cup and rose to his feet with a clever show of reluctance. 'Duty calls, I'm afraid,' he said untruthfully. 'I enjoyed the coffee—and thank you.'

'It isn't the first time you've sampled it,' she said quietly, unable to resist the temptation.

'No?' He raised an eyebrow in enquiry.

She gave an embarrassed little laugh. 'Oh, you've forgotten, of course . . . it was a long time ago. I used to share a flat with Josie Carpenter . . . it was her enthusiasm for nursing that led me to take up the profession.'

He wrinkled his brow in an effort to remember—not that he had ever forgotten Josie but he certainly had no recollection of knowing Sarah Nelson in those long-ago days.

'She brought you to the flat one Sunday,' she reminded him. 'A few months before she gave up nursing.' She tactfully refrained from adding 'to get married' although the thought was in her mind. 'Oh, I don't suppose I made much of an impression,' she added with deceptive lightness. 'You only had eyes for Josie in those days.'

He smiled ruefully. 'Those days are in the dim distant past, I'm afraid . . . I really don't remember any of Josie's friends. But you should have reminded me before—we could have met to talk over old times some evening,' he added courteously.

'Well . . . I was naturally reluctant to bring up Josie's name,' she said quietly. 'In the circumstances . . .'

'Afraid of rubbing salt into old wounds?' he asked, smiling. 'You needn't have worried—Josie and my relationship with her was very soon water under the bridge. At that particular stage in my studies I was a fool to get involved with any girl. We must talk about the past some other time, Nurse . . . but right now I must really be on my way . . .'

Howard closed the door of the sitting-room behind him with a marked sense of relief, leaving Sarah to wonder if she had been wise or foolish to stir up the past . . .

He made his way along the corridor and down the stone staircase with a thoughtful look in his eyes. It was odd but it was not the sudden reminder of Josie that disturbed him . . . it was the abrupt realisation that it was Tiffany Kane's likeness to Josie that antagonised him. It was not so much a physical likeness although Josie had also been pretty and pert and red-headed . . . it was that remarkable, warm friendliness and serene confidence in the liking of others and the lack of ceremony and formality in her dealings with those in authority. It was surprising that he had not recognised the similarity—but then it was a very long time since he had given Josie a thought.

He thought he also understood why Sarah Nelson disliked Tiffany Kane . . . she had been Josie's friend and flat-mate but Josie had always had an unhappy knack for acquiring the men who were originally attracted to her girl-friends. Sarah must have nursed a basic jealousy and resentment for years—and all unconsciously it had turned on a girl who resembled Josie in looks and type.

He wondered idly what had happened to Josie in the intervening years . . . if she had found happiness in her marriage . . . if she had ever thought nostalgically of her nursing days and the fun she had shared with her fellow students . . . if his name and memory ever came to her mind. Not that it could make any difference . . . as he had claimed, it was all water under the bridge. He had been fond of Josie—had certainly believed himself in love with her at the time and suffered agonies of mind and heart because of her inability to resist the attentions of any man who crossed her path. She had kept him dangling for months, playing on his affection and desire, coaxing him to part with money he could ill afford then for perfumes, stockings, cheap jewellery, anything that chanced to catch her eye but was beyond her purse, reproaching him if he did not neglect his studies for the pleasures he could share with her, demanding every form of entertainment and carelessly tossing the taunt that there were other men who would be only too willing to step into his shoes. And it was only later that he learned that they had stepped into his shoes on many occasions . . . only later that he realised what a fool he had been to play into her skilled hands so eagerly.

Josie had been insincere, unkind, cold-hearted

and really rather stupid—but like so many others he had blinded himself to her faults and convinced himself that he loved her and wanted to marry her. At the time he had been shattered by her calm announcement that she was going to marry a man she had known all her life—and he had raged and pleaded and demanded while she listened in smiling, serene silence. It had finally dawned on him that he had never meant anything to her, that she had found him available and useful and willing—and that she had used him as she used any man who fell for her pretty face and empty charm.

It had taken him months to catch up on his studies and to re-establish himself with his superiors as a medical student who really wanted to qualify, who was really interested in medicine, who really could apply himself with energy and enthusiasm and aptitude—but it had taken only a few weeks to realise that it had been only his pride that suffered at Josie's hands. He had been so confident that, of all the men who sought her affections, he must be the one she would choose to marry. He had been so arrogantly scornful of other men when they boasted . . . emptily, he confidently believed . . . of the enjoyment of Josie's company and kisses and caresses. He had been so very blind to her inborn facility for flirtation and so very deaf to the insincerity of her assurances of affection.

Proud and sensitive, the humiliation she had heaped on him had not been easily dismissed or forgotten—and he had been exceptionally wary of involving himself too deeply with any woman until he met Shona . . . and even now he was still wary, reluctant to commit himself, uncertain of the depth and lasting power of his feelings for the beautiful and glamorous star. She was sweet and lovely and desirable . . . and she seemed to prefer him to all the other men she inevitably met and attracted. But always he was conscious of a vague suspicion that Shona might be as insincere and fickle and self-centred as Josie had proved to be . . . and while he could not rid himself of this fear he had no intention of asking her to marry him. He would need to be very sure of the sincerity of any woman's feelings before he decided to make her his wife—and Shona was no exception. And he would need to be very sure that a woman loved him wholeheartedly before he could give his love completely and without reserve . . . Shona had yet to dispel a few doubts . . .

He was pleased to have analysed his dislike for Tiffany Kane. It had worried him a little for the girl had really done nothing to incur his hostility—and he had vaguely felt that he was not giving her a chance to prove whether or not she was as despicable and contemptuous as he believed.

Now he did not doubt at all that the girl was just another Josie . . . an empty-headed flirt who could not be content unless every man she met was at her feet, a selfish, foolish, immature chit who could not be satisfied with the love of the man she had promised to marry and had little or no regard for his feelings or his pride.

He had managed to stir up sufficient righteous

indignation against the girl to justify his dislike by the time he reached the Main Hall and paused to let Joe know that he was leaving the hospital and would not be on call for the rest of the day.

'Very good, sir . . . off to enjoy yourself, are you? Can't say I blame you on a day like this . . . I could do with a tank of cold water up to my neck while I'm behind this desk,' Joe wheezed cheerfully.

Howard checked him over with a professional eye—this heat must be intolerable for a man of Joe's size and it was also pretty bad for a man with his condition. But with two electric fans whirring merrily he was probably better off than the rest of the staff on duty, Howard decided, thinking of the oppressive atmosphere of the wards he had just visited.

'I'll suggest it to the Hospital Committee, Joe,' he promised lightly.

'You do that, sir . . .' And Joe chuckled and wheezed and chuckled again as he looked after the broad, retreating back of the RSO. He approved of Howard Duffy, having known him since his medical student days and never having had cause to complain that the man was arrogant and pompous where he was concerned . . . another mark of favour in Joe's eyes was his circumspection regarding the nurses. Joe was something of a woman-hater—he had an eye for a pretty nurse and exchanged banter happily enough with any one of them who paused at his desk. But the knowledge of his condition had always precluded him from marrying—and he had convinced himself throughout the years that he had no time for marriage and no patience with young men who rushed to the altar with the first girl who captured their fancy. Nor did he look kindly upon medical students who were forever recounting their amorous successes and talking about the latest girl to have caught their interest. Joe had no means of knowing whether or not the RSO indulged in affairs with nurses . . . for his part, he had never seen or heard any evidence to that end.

There had recently been rumours concerning the RSO and a film actress. Joe was addicted to the cinema and wished he had enough courage to ask Mr Duffy if there was any truth in the talk and if so, to name the woman in question. If he was engaged to one of those glamorous young film stars then Joe did not blame him in the least—in his opinion, it was common-sense for a busy surgeon to marry outside his profession. A man had enough of his work without going home to an ex-nurse who expected him to talk of nothing but hospital business . . .

Howard drove away from St Christopher's and headed for the West End, quite unaware of Joe's concern for his personal affairs but his thoughts, oddly enough, following a similar trend. It had needed only one sly comment from a colleague to assure him that, as he had expected, Tiffany Kane had spread the news of his supposed engagement to Shona. But far from being indifferent, he had found himself furiously angry with the girl for her impertinence in discussing his affairs with all and sundry. He was not the kind of man to make a public denial of the gossip that was evidently circulating—but it would give him great pleasure to confront Nurse Kane and demand an explanation for her gossiping tongue and an assurance that she would take steps to kill the rumours. Unfortunately, that would involve pointing out to the girl that he was *not* engaged to Shona . . . and he did not wish Tiffany Kane to be aware of that fact. He felt sure that her belief in his engagement, combined with his determination to give her no cause to fancy that he regretted snubbing her in the first place, had brought about the chill formality that was so much more welcome than her friendly familiarity. She did not like him, of course—but that was preferable to having her like him too much and no doubt some of her recent dislike was due to pique.

Abruptly he realised that his thoughts were of Tiffany Kane—and not for the first time and he cursed the girl for intruding so frequently into his life. It seemed that he could never go anywhere in the hospital without seeing her, these days—and although he set out to ignore her or to treat her with the merest of abrupt courtesies he always discovered later that she was still annoying his thoughts. He ought to be able to dismiss her completely—but sometimes dislike could be as involving an emotion as liking where a woman was concerned. Not that he was prepared to admit that Tiffany Kane was an emotion in his life! She was just an annoying intruder—and he resolutely turned his thoughts to

Shona who would not be expecting him. He had intended to work on his thesis for his Fellowship but it was too warm a day and he needed a break from the demands of his career.

Shona would be at her flat . . . she had assured him that she meant to have a lazy day entirely on her own and enjoy a break from filming. She was making a new film at the moment, a sequel to *Falling Leaves*, working with Justin Amery once more—and Howard found himself wondering idly if Amery had seen any more of Tiffany Kane after that party. For a happily married man, he had seemed quite attracted to the girl, Howard thought cynically—and it was very possible that Tiffany considered him a more rewarding conquest than a mere surgeon who had made it very clear that he was not interested in her favours. It was obvious that Tiffany would not concern herself unduly with the fact that Amery was married—like most girls of her type, she probably never considered anything but her own wishes and desires and interests . . . and when in heaven's name had he begun thinking of that wretched little junior as 'Tiffany,' he demanded of himself hotly, once more making the effort to concentrate on the traffic and his impatience to be with Shona again . . .

CHAPTER NINE

As soon as Shona Sinclair had signed the contract for *Falling Leaves* she had taken a lease on a luxury flat in Park Lane. Howard had grown used to the drive across London from the hospital but he could still be irked by the traffic, as he was this afternoon when it seemed that the world and his wife was on the roads.

But at last he drove into the forecourt of the huge white block of flats and glanced automatically upwards as he locked the car door before turning towards the entrance. Shona's flat was on the fifth floor and provided an expansive view of the park. She did not like the present heat wave and, as he had expected, the window blinds were lowered.

Within moments, he was walking out of the lift and along the thickly carpeted corridor to Shona's flat. He rang the bell and waited, a faint smile curving his lips as he thought of her astonishment at sight of him. Because he wished to surprise her, he had deliberately not given his usual, familiar ring on the bell.

She was slow to answer the door and a faint frown replaced the smile as he rang again . . . he would be the surprised one if Shona had decided to go out, after all—for she had assured him she would be at home and a hot, sultry day like this one was not likely to tempt her out of doors.

The door opened almost reluctantly and Shona stared at him . . . not so much with surprise as dismay, he thought immediately.

'Were you resting?' he asked, a little contritely as he walked past her into the flat, very much at home as always. He smiled down at her lovely, slightly flushed face, bare of make-up, and touched her rumpled, blue-black hair with an affectionate hand. 'You look very pretty,' he said lightly.

'I didn't expect you, Howard,' she said slowly, uncertainly.

'No, I know . . . I told you that I would be working but I changed my mind. Am I unwelcome?' he added teasingly, confidently.

She turned towards the open door of the lounge. 'You'd better come in,' she said ungraciously—and quite belatedly for he was close on her heels.

Howard paused, his eyes hardening as he took in the recumbent figure of the man on the settee, the drinks on the table, the overflowing ashtrays and the general disorder of the room. There was little light with the blinds drawn but enough for him to recognise Giles Cavendish.

Giles raised his glass in welcome. 'Hallo there, old man . . . join us in a drink?' His voice was slightly slurred.

Shona moved swiftly across the room and almost snatched the glass from his hand. 'You've had enough, Giles,' she said, venting her anger on him.

He lay back on the cushions, grinning. 'What's

the matter, darling . . . double-dated yourself? I was here first, remember—tell him to go to hell!'

Howard involuntarily clenched his fists and took a step forward. He was sick with anger and humiliation and a burning disappointment. He knew the violent impulse to catch the other man by the scruff of his neck and throw him out of the flat but in the midst of his anger he was sane enough to realise that Cavendish was there by Shona's invitation.

Shona came towards him anxiously. It had suited her very well to have two men dancing attendance on her for the past weeks but the last thing she had wanted was for Howard to learn of her relationship with Giles—and she did not relish the thought of them coming to blows because of her duplicity.

'You said you would be working,' she reminded Howard petulantly. 'You know how I hate my own company—Giles happened to drop in for a few minutes and I asked him to stay for lunch. How could I know that you'd turn up unexpectedly?'

'You couldn't,' he agreed, his tone and gaze icy.

'You're so unpredictable,' she accused.

'Maybe . . . but disloyalty has never been one of my faults,' he told her cuttingly.

She took a cigarette from the box on the table. 'Oh, don't be smug!' she snapped irritably. 'Disloyalty indeed—because I have lunch with another man? I thought you weren't the jealous type,' she added sneeringly.

'I'm not . . . I'm merely proud and I don't like the idea of my girl deceiving me behind my back, Shona.'

Giles laughed unpleasantly. 'Your girl, old man? Shona is anyone's girl—aren't you, my sweet?'

She rounded on him furiously. 'Why don't you shut up and get out?'

'Because I'm enjoying this little drama—hammy though it is,' he retorted smoothly.

'I think you'd be wise to do as you're told . . . before I put you out,' Howard warned him menacingly.

Giles chuckled softly. 'But Shona doesn't really want me to go, you know . . . you don't know her very well, do you, old man? If I went she'd have the wool pulled over your eyes again in five minutes . . . and to tell the truth I'm rather tired of dodging you. It's time you learned that your day is done, Duffy—and it might help you to realise it if I point out that it was yesterday morning when I dropped in and stayed for lunch. Shona finds me so attractive that she just can't bear to part with me, you see.' He rose leisurely to his feet, a tall, indolent man, and slipped an arm about Shona's waist with a possessive hint of intimacy. She wriggled free of him, her face flaming with annoyance.

'Why on earth did you have to tell him?' she flared.

He looked down at her steadily. 'As I said, I'm tired of dodging your doctor friend—and I have my pride too. I won't go on sharing you with him or any other man, Shona. The choice is yours.'

Howard said quietly, vehemently: 'There is no question of choice . . . it seems that Shona has already made up her mind. I'm sorry I disturbed you but I'm leaving immediately.'

He turned on his heel and strode from the room. Shona glared at Giles and then ran after him, catching his arm as he raised his hand to the latch.

'Wait, Howard . . . !'

He looked down at her coldly. 'Don't bother, Shona . . . I really didn't need that insolent puppy's revelations to realise the truth about you. I think I've always suspected that you're just like any other woman . . . selfish, spoiled and caring for no one but yourself. What you want you take—and to hell with everyone else!'

Her hand fell from his arm. She was pale now where she had been so flushed. 'You make it all seem so beastly,' she said in a low reproachful voice.

'Isn't it?' he retorted.

'Giles was too blunt . . . it wasn't quite as he claimed, you know.'

'He stayed the night with you, didn't he?'

She shrugged. 'You attach so much importance to that? Doesn't it mean anything that I've given you so much during the past three years? I loved you, Howard—and you never had time to fall in love with me! You're in love with your work—and no woman can compete with that! I'm tired of taking second place, Howard—tired of being fitted in when you weren't too busy! Giles Cavendish! A mere boy! Haven't you enough sense to realise why I encouraged him in the first place—or why he stayed here last night? You were going to be busy all the weekend . . . on duty all day yesterday, working on your thesis today . . . and I'm supposed to kick my heels and wait until you find the time for me. I was so bored, so miserable, so resentful when Giles turned up here yesterday . . . can you really blame me for welcoming him with open arms?'

'Was it the first time you'd welcomed him so warmly?' he asked coldly, suspiciously. 'He spoke of having to dodge me . . . it can't have been so difficult if I've always been too busy for you, Shona.'

'So I've been out with him a few times? That isn't a crime!' she said angrily. 'He's attractive and amusing . . . and he's in love with me! You didn't even want to be engaged to me . . . remember that night when we went to Rebecca Waring's party— when I met Giles? Oh, I was stupid—I thought I might force your hand if I claimed that we were engaged. Instead you pointed out that most women waited for the man to propose before telling the world that he wanted to marry her—so much you cared for my feelings! I knew then that you didn't love me in the least . . . and when Giles telephoned me the next day and suggested a date I didn't hesitate. You only have yourself to blame, Howard!'

'In that case, there is no point in continuing this conversation,' he said indifferently. 'Your young friend must be getting impatient, Shona—I've kept you from his arms quite long enough.'

She looked up at him, her lips quivering slightly. 'Will I see you again, Howard?'

He stared at her in complete astonishment. 'Do you really imagine that's likely? I haven't the slightest desire to see you again . . . I'm not impressed by your pleas or your claims. You haven't given me so very much, Shona—not as much as you've given that amateur Don Juan, if it comes to that! It seems to me that you've come off best during the entire life of our friendship—as women like you always do.' He opened the door of the flat. 'And it's running true to type to turn sentimental as soon as you realise that an affair is irrevocably ended.'

'I loved you, Howard,' she repeated quietly.

'Perhaps you did . . . as much as you could love anyone. But when I wouldn't conform to your expectations of a lover, I rather think that irritation and resentment and impatience replaced the finer feeling. You were out of love with me a long time ago, Shona—and that's why I haven't the slightest compunction in breaking with you . . . although I'm willing to admit that the break was forced on me. I didn't wish it—I might even have married you.'

'Very magnanimous of you!' she threw at him bitterly, fiercely. 'When? Ten, twenty, thirty years from now? When you could spare the time from your work? When you needed a presentable wife to act as hostess for you? When you'd realised that the kind of woman you're looking for just doesn't exist because no woman could live up to your fantastic standards? Face facts, Howard, for heaven's sake! You're arrogant and demanding and as selfish as they come—and you're hoping to find a doormat who'll never have an opinion or thought or idea of her own, who won't mind playing second fiddle to a pair of surgical gloves and who'll be perfectly content to be there when you want her and to efface herself when you don't! I hope you never find her—you'd make her life a misery and a torment!'

His lips tightening and his eyes cold and steely, he walked out of the flat and down the corridor to the lift without a backward glance . . . and Shona slammed the door with all the force she could muster before she burst into angry, painful sobs.

Giles lounged in the doorway, watching her, his own eyes a little hard and angry. They had been so engrossed in telling each other home truths that neither had noticed him, an interested ear to every word.

Shona pushed past him without a word and threw herself on the settee in a tumult of tears . . . and, because he was desperately in love with her, heaven help him, he hesitated only a moment before going to her and drawing her into his strong and comforting arms. She resisted him angrily at first, blaming him entirely for the loss of the man who had once meant so much to her and might again if he had seemed to care for her only a little with the passing of time. Then, as Giles continued to hold her close and murmur foolish, soothing endearments, she relaxed against him—and soon she was clinging to him, giving her lips to him feverishly as though she would blot out all thought and memory of Howard Duffy.

Howard drove towards Marble Arch, turned into

the Bayswater Road and headed for Sheperds Bush and the Western Avenue, all without conscious thought. He was burning with anger and a violent desire to hurt someone, anyone as a retaliation for the pain that had just been inflicted on him.

Oh, he knew well enough that his pride rather than his heart had taken the blow . . . he did not love Shona but she had meant quite a lot in his life for three years and it was the humiliation of discovering that a man ten years his junior had replaced him within a few weeks of their meeting.

This was not new to him, he thought bitterly, as all the old, familiar feelings soared through his taut being. Josie had thrown his affection and loyalty and trust in his face all those years ago . . . he should have known better than to give them a second time to any woman. It might so easily have been his love that Shona had rejected so carelessly . . . and he supposed there was something to be said for an inability to love with ease and eagerness.

He would probably never love any woman. Perhaps he did lack the ability to love—or perhaps he did ask too much of any woman. His mouth twisted wryly as Shona's accusations resounded in his ears . . . could there be any truth in them? Was he looking for the kind of woman she had depicted? Was he so arrogant and demanding and selfish—or was it rather the truth that no woman in the world knew the meaning of honesty and loyalty and understanding?

Was it simply a matter of always being attracted to the wrong type of woman . . . or were there no other types in existence? After Josie, he had determined that he would never make the same mistake a second time—and yet he had! Josie . . . Shona—two peas from the same pod, he thought cynically, and it seemed he had not learned a thing from the first disastrous affair. Well, he was older and wiser now . . . a better pupil, no doubt! He had learned at last that a man could not have two loves in his life—and surgery possessed him more completely than any woman possibly could. In future, he would stick to surgery and cut out the women . . . !

Abruptly he realised that he was heading in the wrong direction—and at the first opportunity he turned the car. A faintly scornful smile touched his mouth . . . he had been heading in the wrong direction for a long time but now he was on the right road. He would concentrate on getting his Fellowship and, later, his Professorship if fortune smiled on him. Ambition left no room for love and marriage in his life—hadn't he always known that? So why had he continued to search for the one woman to match his ideal, the one woman he could love beyond anything else, even surgery . . . ?

He drove fast and well, unconsciously taking care for he was a good and conscientious driver . . . and it was not so very long before he was within easy reach of St Christopher's, his flat and his thesis. It was just past four o'clock as he slowed down for the zebra crossing outside the hospital—and he stiffened in his seat as he recognised a familiar mass of red hair.

Tiffany was out of uniform, wearing her cool

dress of primrose silk and high-heeled shoes, and despite the heat she looked fresh and young and very pretty. She darted across the road and turned to smile her thanks at the courteous motorist—and her smile faded as she met Howard Duffy's eyes.

He looked at her with deliberate blankness, let in the clutch and drove on—and Tiffany looked after the car with a vague sensation of pain because he could not even respond with courtesy or pleasantry to her smile. She gave a little shrug to dismiss the feeling and walked on, heading for the underground station. She was on her way to meet Justin Amery and she banished the thought of the surgeon with the more pleasant anticipation of meeting the actor once more.

They had met several times since that first encounter at Rebecca's party and their friendship had developed into a mutually warm affection despite the difference in their ages and the totally different ways of life.

Tiffany had lunched with him, spent a day at the film studios where he was currently working, enjoyed a concert at the Festival Hall in his company and this evening she was meeting Justin and his wife and going with them to a party in Chelsea. She had not yet met Helen Amery and she was a little nervous although Justin had described his wife so often and so lovingly to her that she felt as though she knew Helen very well. She naturally hoped that Helen would like her and understand why Justin had carried a casual meeting into friendship—but, being Tiffany, it did not occur to her that Justin's wife might be jealous or suspicious of that friendship.

She was a little naive at times—or perhaps it was merely her innate innocence that blinded her to the petty interpretations that most people would place on an association of any kind between a mature film star and a young girl, particularly when the man happened to be married.

She liked and trusted Justin Amery . . . there had never been a word exchanged that his wife could not have heard and the only physical contact had been the merest touch of his hand beneath her elbow to guide her across a road or a foyer or between the tables of a restaurant.

Justin's feeling for Tiffany Kane bordered very closely on the avuncular . . . she might have been a favourite niece whose company he enjoyed. Certainly it never entered his head that she was an attractive and desirable young girl although he was too worldly wise not to fear for her reputation and his own if they were seen too much together. For that very reason, he had seen to it that Helen went with them that evening to the party that was being thrown by an artist friend. He had told Helen about his meeting with the young nurse, spoken of her warmly and freely but in a way that assured Helen Amery that she had nothing to fear from this unknown girl—and he had been perfectly open about his further meetings with Tiffany.

Helen reacted to the friendly, natural, sweet-natured girl much as others did . . . and before the evening came to an end she was suggesting to Justin that they should invite Tiffany to spend a weekend with them. Seldom at her ease at parties of any kind, Helen had enjoyed the evening with Tiffany, finding her exactly as she had imagined, had been content to spend most of the time talking to her about her children, her home in Kent, Justin's good qualities and unspoiled temperament and in discovering that they had many mutual interests and tastes.

They drove her back to the hospital despite her assurance that the journey did not bother her—still comparatively early, a little before eleven, because they would not leave their children to the care of a baby-sitter for too many hours.

Tiffany waved them away outside the hospital and then turned to make her way across the small, well-lit park to the Nurses' Home, glancing up at the darkened bulk of the hospital building with its occasional splashes of light as she walked briskly under the clear, starry sky . . .

CHAPTER TEN

As she neared one of the benches that a thoughtful Hospital Committee had provided at intervals throughout the park, a man rose to his feet, dropping his cigarette and stepping on it.

Tiffany jumped nervously and gave a stifled little exclamation. She had been completely absorbed in recollections of the evening and the man's sudden movement had startled her with its unexpected abruptness.

He turned quickly towards her—and her heart leaped into her throat for there had recently been complaints by some of the nurses that a man had tried to molest them at night in this very park. Only her sense of pride and dignity . . . and perhaps her high heels . . . prevented her from breaking into a run but she certainly quickened her steps.

'I'm afraid I startled you,' Howard Duffy said ruefully, not immediately recognising the girl who began to back away at his approach and then hurried forward to pass him.

Tiffany paused, recognising his voice and then the man as she dared to look at him fully. 'Oh, it's you,' she said thankfully.

Her words triggered off a memory . . . a night under the stars when this same girl had made the same remark but with a totally different note in her voice. It was evidently a night for coincidences, he thought wryly, for this was the second time he had seen her within a few short hours—and neither time had been on a hospital ward.

'Good evening,' he said stiffly, preparing to walk on.

She smiled up at him warmly, so relieved was she to meet a familiar face after her sudden spasm of nerves. 'I thought you were the Lurking Lecher,' she said impulsively.

He grimaced. 'Yes, I've heard about that business . . . damnably unpleasant. You haven't been molested in any way, I hope.'

'No . . . but I must admit that I haven't walked across the park on my own at night since I was told about him.'

'I'll walk with you,' he said abruptly—moved more by an impulse of chivalry than anything else. 'I haven't seen anyone lurking—except a courting couple. But one never knows.'

'Thank you,' she murmured, so taken aback by the unexpected offer that she scarcely knew what to say—and scarcely liked to refuse.

They walked for a few moments in silence. Then, impelled by courtesy, he said lightly, not wishing to convey real interest: 'You're out late, Nurse.'

She looked up at him quickly, wondering if he queried the validity of her late return. 'Oh, I have a pass,' she assured him. 'Approved and signed by Matron.'

He was abruptly reminded of his medical student days and he replied involuntarily: 'Then you won't need to climb through the bathroom window, will you?'

Tiffany chuckled. 'Not this time.'

He smiled. It was an instinctive response to the gay, lilting merriment of her soft voice. 'But you have on occasions!'

'Like George Washington, I can't tell a lie—but I've never been caught so you won't turn informer and report me to Matron, will you?'

His eyes suddenly narrowed. Was that a deliberate taunt to remind him of their clash on Adeline Ward earlier in the day? Perhaps not, he decided, as she looked up at him with a warm smile and he met the friendliness of her quick glance. In that moment, it seemed rather unfair and certainly difficult to suspect her of petty malice.

'Where were you going in such a hurry earlier this evening?' he asked carelessly. 'I wish all users of zebra crossings would take a tip from you and cross the road so swiftly.'

'Oh, I'm always in a hurry,' she retorted lightly. 'My friends always tell me that I couldn't dawdle to save my life. I was on my way to a party actually.'

'You enjoy parties, don't you?' There was the merest hint of nostalgia in his voice for the days when he had been young enough and enthusiastic enough to hasten to a party.

It was Tiffany's turn to wonder swiftly if he was taunting her with a reminder of the party at which they had met for the first time outside the precincts of the hospital . . . he had accused her that night of making a play for Justin and she had been so furious with him. What would his reaction be if he learned that she had seen Justin on several occasions since that night, she thought wryly . . . probably the same as that of many others, a petty, nasty minded, suspicious reaction to the discovery that a married man and a girl so much his junior liked each other sufficiently to be friends without spoiling that friendship with stupid, unnecessary emotions.

'That depends on the company,' she said airily.

He raised a quizzical eyebrow. 'Even at your age?' he said, amused.

She tilted her chin sharply. 'I'm not such an infant . . . I shall be twenty-three very soon.'

'A great age,' he said solemnly.

She glanced at him suspiciously. 'You're mocking me,' she said reproachfully.

'I'm probably just jealous.' He grinned. 'I shall never see twenty-three again . . . or thirty-three, if it comes to that!'

'Oh . . . Methuselah!' she said with mock impatience.

'I feel like him at times, too,' he assured her, half-seriously. They had paused outside the Nurses' Home, both of them perhaps too relieved to find that they could talk to each other without acrimony if only once in the course of their association to be eager to part. He was startled when she raised a hand to his face, running her finger-tips along his chin. 'What are you doing?' he asked, more abruptly than he meant, catching her hand.

'Trying to find your beard,' she retorted, teasing him. 'You conceal it so well!'

He realised that he still possessed her hand . . . momentarily he was at a loss to know what to do with it. It seemed too abrupt, too unkind to release it as though it were a hot coal yet he had no wish to retain her cool, slim fingers in his own.

'You wouldn't dare to talk to me in that fashion on the ward,' he chided lightly, pressing her fingers briefly before releasing them.

'You don't give me much opportunity to talk to you at all,' she could not resist pointing out. 'Which brings me to something I've had on my mind for a long time,' she went on, finding the courage to tackle him now that he seemed in a reasonable, almost likeable mood. 'Tell me, Mr Duffy—what did I ever do to offend you? If I knew I could apologise . . . and perhaps we could stop being at loggerheads every time we meet.'

'Are we at loggerheads now?' he countered, startled and a little dismayed by her abrupt attack and suddenly finding that he could not remember how or when she had done anything to make him feel that she was so detestable and despicable.

'No . . . and that surprises me a little,' she admitted, a frown in her eyes. 'For the first time I can talk to you as though you were a human being . . . and you aren't treating me as though I were something the cat had just deposited at your feet.'

He laughed involuntarily at her description of his manner in the past towards her. 'Oh come . . . I've never been that bad!' he protested.

'Oh yes, you have! And I wish I knew why . . . won't you tell me?' she asked gently, prettily.

'I don't think *I* even know why,' he admitted, smiling down at her ... a smile so warm, so friendly, so appealing that her heart lurched abruptly and she was suddenly aflame from top to toe with a heat that seared in her veins.

'Then it *was* just a case of Dr Fell,' she blurted for want of something to say, shaken to the depths of her being by the strange chemical reaction of her heart and body to his smile and the warmth in his voice.

'But you don't like me either,' he pointed out quietly. 'Do you have a reason that you can put into words?'

Tiffany shook her head, every harsh word and icy glance and indifferent avoidal completely forgotten for the moment.

'Then perhaps we ought to cry pax,' he suggested easily ... even while he wondered what the devil he was doing, lingering under the stars with a junior nurse and going out of his way to make friends with her when he had perfectly good cause for avoiding all women in the future—and particularly a girl like this one who had been proved to be a wayward and irresponsible flirt.

Tiffany held out her hand to him immediately, a little more mistress of herself now that her heart had steadied and her blood had cooled. Later she would wonder at that odd sensation and try to analyse its cause ... for the moment she preferred not to think about it!'

'Justin *will* be pleased!' she exclaimed, so delighted was she by his offer of friendship. 'He could never understand why we detested each other so much when he likes us both.'

He was abruptly unaware of her outstretched hand. 'Justin?' he demanded coldly. 'Justin Amery, do you mean?'

'Of course.' Her ignored hand fell back to her side and she stared up at him, puzzled.

'What the devil do you both mean by discussing me in the first place?' he flared, seized by a sudden, inexplicable anger.

Tiffany was completely bewildered. 'It was inevitable that you would be mentioned,' she said drily. 'After all, he is a friend of yours, Mr Duffy—and he knows that we both work at Kit's. Naturally he speaks of you on occasions.'

'Occasions!' he repeated. 'Do you mean that you've been seeing him since that night? Although I warned you not to make a fool of yourself!'

His voice was taut with anger—and Tiffany's own fierce temper leaped to life. 'Yes, you warned me!' she flared. 'I remember that! And what right did you have to say such things to me? It was none of your business then—and it's none of your business now! Yes, I've been seeing Justin . . . why shouldn't I? I'm fond of him—I believe that he's fond of me!'

'He's married!' Howard snapped bitingly.

'So he must never speak to anyone but his wife?' she jeered.

'You've been going out with him? You stupid little fool! What are you after? Your name in the gossip columns . . . ?' He seized her by the shoulders, holding her in a grip that bruised. 'Haven't you any sense? Any thought for your reputation—or the risk of involving Kit's in a scandal? Do you think Kit's will continue to train a girl who cares so little for her good name or the name of the hospital that she runs around with a married man? Oh, it isn't just that he's married . . . he also happens to be a famous name—is that what attracted you?'

Tiffany, shaking with anger and humiliation, wrenched herself free from his fierce hands. 'Why should you concern yourself with my reputation—or my job? Allow me to take care of my affairs for myself, if you please,' she told him icily. 'Yes, I've been going out with him . . . my life is my own. I don't have to answer to anyone . . . and certainly not to you, RSO or not! You're not in authority over me! I've been out with him tonight—to that party—if you must know! But I still don't see that it's any business of yours!'

He slapped her face. His hand had moved entirely of its own volition. But even when his mind realised the enormity of the action he did not regret it. He had never been so angry in his life—never felt more keenly that someone had to take steps to prevent a young girl from completely ruining her life with a youthful, foolish insane infatuation. He was almost outside himself with anger—and he did not regret that slap in the least as he looked or rather glared down at her stunned, incredulous, stricken face, her hand to her smarting cheek and tears of pain in her eyes.

'You must be mad!' The vehement accusation was torn from her fiercely.

'Someone has to knock some sense into you!'

'It isn't your place or your concern or your right! I won't have you interfering in my affairs . . . I won't stand for violence from you or anyone. I shall sue you for assault!' The words poured from her as she stood, trembling, almost in tears, shocked and bewildered and furious, taut and tense before him. 'That won't do *your* reputation or *your* career any good, will it?'

She turned away, so abruptly, so violently, that her heel turned and wrenched away from the shoe. Raging, Tiffany snatched her shoes from her feet and turned on him once more, small, fierce, proud and outraged.

'And I shall claim damages for these!' she threw at him, thrusting the shoes towards him.

He caught her wrist, calmer now, a little frightened by what he had done and said . . . not because of her threat but because it was the first time in his life that he had lost complete control of his temper and he simply could not understand why it had happened.

'Will you let me go!' she stormed.

'In a moment,' he said quietly.

'I loathe, detest and despise you!' she told him in low, fierce, contemptuous tones.

'I'm sorry,' he said abruptly—and with a great deal of difficulty. 'I lost my temper.'

'Your personal feelings intruded once more!' she sneered. 'I don't accept your apology—and it certainly doesn't make me change my mind about suing you. You'll learn that it doesn't pay to lose your temper—or to question me about my social life!'

'All right . . . all right!' he snapped. 'I had no right to say and do any of it . . . I admit that. Will you listen to me and stop struggling!' he added impatiently as she tried once more to free herself from his clasp.

'Take your hands off me!' She was almost crying with temper.

'In a moment,' he repeated. 'Listen, Tiffany— I'm only thinking of you. Justin Amery can take care of himself but I'd like to tear him to shreds for taking advantage of a silly girl's fascination for the glamour of show business! For God's sake, don't make the mistake of thinking that he means anything but the careless enjoyment of a brief affair. He's happy with his wife—he adores his children. He wouldn't break up his marriage for any girl, believe me!' He was striving to make her see reason, completely convinced that her fury stemmed from a feeling that he had violated her affection for Amery. 'Don't make a fool of yourself,' he went on urgently. 'You wouldn't be happy with a man like Amery if he did want to marry you— and what was wrong with your fiancé that you felt the need to run after other men? What does he say to all this?' He realised that he was talking to her like a Dutch uncle—but he told himself with absolute sincerity that his concern for her was born of a consideration of her youth and naivety and childish folly.

'If you're talking about Michael Gilroy—I'm not engaged to him and never have been and never will be! Now let me go—and stop interfering! I'm a free agent and I do as I like!'

He released her wrist and she massaged it instinctively for it ached from the pressure of his steely fingers. 'Very well . . . on your own head be it,' he said quietly, heavily.

She threw him a glance of contempt. She stooped to retrieve her shoes which had fallen to the ground during their heated and amazing battle of wills. 'Don't ever dare to speak to me again,' she said through clenched teeth.

'Keep away from Amery!' he called after her relentlessly.

She turned to glare at him. 'I'm spending a weekend with him soon—if it interests you!' she retorted, too carried away with her temper to care for complete truth. She ran across the forecourt, wincing as her stockinged feet found stones on the ground and reached the safety of the building with a feeling of profound thankfulness and relief . . .

Howard stood staring at the building for a few minutes. Then he turned and walked away swiftly, cursing the impulse which had brought him out into the night air for a quiet cigarette and a brief relaxation from his books and his thesis. He had been a fool. He realised that only too well. He had involved himself in something that simply was nothing to do with him . . . and Tiffany Kane had every justification for carrying out the threats she had made. What on earth had possessed him? He had not been drinking or overworking. He had absolutely no excuse to offer. He had been carried away by a righteous indignation, a horror of standing by and watching a fellow human-being make a fool of herself, an impulse to avert the disaster she was deliberately inviting, if he could.

And what good had he done? He had probably done his reputation and his career irreparable harm—and such was the irony of life it was very likely that she would extricate herself from the affair with Amery before it could become a scandal and neither her reputation nor her career would suffer.

He ran a hand through his dark hair. It was too late for apprehension and dismay and a heartfelt wish that he had never offered his escort across the park to a girl he had never liked and religiously avoided as much as possible.

Odd . . . they had been getting on quite well, considering their natural antipathy. He had almost warmed to her . . . more than that, he *had* warmed to her, had wondered if he had misjudged her, had found her unaffected and appealing and rather attractive—youthful, vivacious, pretty, amusing and he had known the swift impulse to wipe out all the antagonism and hostility and replace it with some form of friendship . . . inasmuch as the RSO of Kit's and a junior nurse could become involved in friendship.

The mere mention of Justin Amery had set him raging with anger—and he simply did not know why the man's name, in association with Tiffany Kane, should have acted like a red rag to a bull. Her personal life was entirely her own affair. If she chose to indulge in a foolish association with a married man—then who was he to try to prevent or end it? What did it matter to him, in heaven's name? He scarcely knew the girl—did not even like her. It was nothing to him what she did with her life, what mistakes she made, what scandals she evoked with her behaviour.

He *must* be mad! Tiffany was right to accuse him of insanity . . . a temporary insanity, certainly. And he had absolutely no idea how he was going to get himself out of the mess that was certain to develop from this night's events.

It had been a foul day from beginning to end, he thought bitterly. It had begun with that stupid contretemps on Adeline with Tiffany Kane, continued in the humiliating episode at Shona's flat which had made it almost impossible for him to concentrate on his thesis that evening—and it had been nicely rounded off with his disastrous encounter with a girl who was determined to go to the devil regardless of anyone's attempts to stop her . . .

CHAPTER ELEVEN

TIFFANY closed the door of her room with a snap of finality. That was that! That was a perfectly enjoyable evening utterly ruined by a chance encounter with the one person in the world she loathed and despised and would gladly see banished to the ends of the earth!

She moved slowly to the mirror and stared at her pale, bewildered face as though she expected to find the marks of his fingers still imprinted on her cheek. It seemed incredible, absolutely unbelievable, that he had dared to do such a thing—and she burned all over with renewed indignation and resentment.

Abruptly she turned away and began to undress with hands that still trembled from the shock and distress of the past half hour. She was cold and frightened and completely bewildered by the young surgeon's behaviour.

Hastily she slipped between the sheets and curled into a tight, taut ball, hands clenched and a sick dismay in the pit of her stomach. She had never met with violence at anyone's hands before—and she had never known that any man's anger could be quite so violent and unexpected and inexplicable.

She reproached herself for dwelling on the episode . . . forget it and try to sleep, she admonished herself sternly, determined to put him out of her mind. But sleep was more than elusive . . . it simply had no intention of enfolding her at all until she had marshalled her thoughts and emotions and found a degree of calmness.

With a sigh, she sat up in bed and switched on the light. Of all men in the world, Howard Duffy was surely the strangest, she thought wearily. Earlier in the day, meeting on the ward, he had treated her with cold contempt . . . but she had grown used to such treatment from him and scarcely expected anything else. She had been quite convinced that she would not welcome any change in his attitude at this late date. And then she had met him by chance on her way across the park . . . he had been courteous, considerate, even friendly—they had talked and laughed together without any hint of their usual antagonism to each other. Then . . . Tiffany's face flamed as she recalled that moment when he had looked down at her with gentle, smiling warmth and she had reacted as though he were the most exciting, interesting, attractive man she had ever met instead of the most detestable. It had all been very odd . . . her heart had apparently tumbled upside down in that brief moment and she had been oblivious to everything but his nearness and the smile in his eyes and the excitement in her veins. Tiffany felt that it was as inexplicable as his unexpected explosion of anger that had dismayed her as much as the blow she had received.

Why should he be so concerned, so angry because she had admitted to seeing Justin since that first meeting? Whatever she did could not really concern him in the least, should certainly not arouse his anger! Perhaps it was natural that he should fear any breath of scandal attaching to a Kit's nurse . . . but why should he automatically assume that she would involve herself in a scandal? His opinion of her must be low in the extreme, she thought bitterly—and was appalled by the slow, crushing vice that caught at her heart at the thought.

Her eyes widened and she stared blindly across the room. Why should it matter that he thought so ill of her? Why should she care for his good opinion or his liking or his friendship—or anything else for that matter? But she did care, she realised miserably—and she did not want this man of all men to despise and reject and ignore her!

That very first snub had hurt her more than she had cared to admit at the time, she realised abruptly—but he had been a virtual stranger and it should not have crossed her mind a second time. Oh, she had seen him about the hospital—she had heard the other girls talking about the handsome surgeon who had been trained at Kit's, taken his MRCS degree and then tried his hand at general practice before returning to Kit's as a surgeon. She had probably glanced at him with faint interest but there had never been any occasion to speak to him until that fateful day when she had hurried after him with his fountain pen and apparently offended his dignity by the friendliness which he had construed as unwelcome familiarity from a junior nurse. Perhaps she had unconsciously seized on the opportunity to speak to him, to catch him before he left the ward, to make some kind of contact with the man whose work she admired . . . perhaps the warning of her fellow-nurses that he was a difficult, proud and demanding man with whom it was always advisable to tread softly had acted as a challenge to her innate conviction that no one was unapproachable or unfriendly at heart. Perhaps she had always made friends too easily . . . perhaps she was too confident that no one could resist her light-hearted friendliness.

It was not surprising that Howard Duffy had thought her forward and vain—perhaps he had even condemned her friendliness as an attempt at flirtation. After all, some girls did go to great lengths to attract the doctors and surgeons, to create opportunities for private conversation and flirtation and, not knowing Tiffany, how could he be expected to differentiate on sight between a girl who merely sought and offered friendship and a girl who openly sought and offered the fleeting excitement of casual flirtation.

Then the party at Rebecca's house . . . when he had accused her of making a play for Justin. Surely that confirmed that he had already made up his mind that she was an incorrigible flirt? As a friend, one might expect him to try to protect Justin from further gossip about his affairs which might have led to trouble with his marriage—hence the warning he had given Tiffany that night and the further evidence of his contempt for her . . . which could only seem proof that he had no time or respect for supposed flirts who sought to make a conquest of every man who came in their way.

Oh, things were falling into place, Tiffany thought sadly—and now, by her own words, she had convinced him that she was neither worthy of his respect or his liking. She had thrown stupid, defiant admissions at his head—allowed him to believe that she was having an affair with Justin Amery . . . and because Justin was his friend, he had naturally been so angry that he had lost complete control of his self-possession.

Yet that did not explain his urgent appeal to her common-sense and understanding of a world in which men like Justin, of his age and standing, did not throw over a happy marriage for a passing fancy. He had honestly seemed more concerned for her than for Justin—and he had used her first name for the first time in their entire association, she recalled with a tiny pang. She had scarcely realised that he remembered what it was—and even in her anger she had thrilled to the sweet, soft sound of her name on his lips.

She was a fool . . . a stupid, inexperienced, blind little fool. Facing the truth squarely, despite the pain and humiliation and despair which almost made her writhe, she knew that she had committed the crass folly of falling in love with Howard Duffy. Even in totally different circumstances . . . had he liked her a little, shown her respect and courtesy and warmth during the past weeks since their first exchange of words, there could still have been not the slightest hope that he was really interested in a junior nurse. Only the strangest of coincidences had provided a social occasion for them to meet . . . normally, the RSO and a second-year-nurse would never meet outside the hospital buildings. Normally, he would hesitate to show interest in any of the student nurses for such things were frowned on by the hospital authorities.

But how could she love him when he had never given her the least cause to like him? Or almost never, she amended honestly, recalling the pleasure of his company, the attractions of his smile and voice and manner, the complete contrast to the cold, formal, arrogant surgeon who could scarcely bring himself to speak to her. But that change in him had lasted so short a time . . . and she knew now that she had been falling in love with him for weeks! That was perhaps the strangest part of all—that she could learn to love a man who had seemed so unkind, unreasonable, detestable and hostile. But only to her, she reminded herself, remembering the charming smile, the easy courtesies, the warmth of manner he had bestowed on everyone else within her sight and hearing on so many occasions.

It did not really matter how or why—she loved him and there was more pain than pleasure to be gained from the knowledge, she realised, thrusting a hand against her mouth to stifle a sob of anguish. Tears and self-recriminations and an ardent desire to erase the past weeks were all in vain—and she would have to learn to live with her love for the man who would never think of her without contempt, never meet her without an icy stiffening of his manner, never wish to speak to her except when it proved unavoidable because of their mutual profession . . .

Tiffany was convinced that she would never sleep that night . . . but she was abruptly aroused from a heavy, dream-filled slumber by a knock on her door. She rolled over and glanced at the clock beside her bed—and with an effort she threw back the bedclothes and swung her feet to the floor.

Jess met her in the corridor and noted with concern and surprise the heavy-lidded eyes with the dark shadows beneath, the unusual pallor of her friend's small face, the general listlessness of her demeanour.

'You must have had a late night!' she exclaimed. 'You and your parties!'

Tiffany forced herself to smile. 'Oh, it wasn't so very late,' she protested—but the last thing she wanted was to talk about the previous evening . . . or to talk at all, for that matter. She wanted to be left to brood, to mourn for her lost and irretrievable heart, she thought miserably . . . and immediately knew a flicker of her usual sense of humour. There was no point in all this heavy drama, she told herself firmly . . . and made the effort to talk to Jess during breakfast although she did not have any appetite or interest in the meal.

She was unaware of the curious glances, the buzz of excitement and the furtive whispers of a group of nurses at the further end of the table . . . and Jess was too concerned with her friend's obvious and worrying state of mind to notice anyone else. Tiffany would have been even more shocked and distressed if she could have heard the conversation. She had thought at the time that it was fortunate that no one chanced to interrupt or overhear her violent quarrel with the RSO . . . she did not know that two of her colleagues, arriving home from a dance, had witnessed the briefly intimate and absorbing few moments which heralded their mutual fury. They had seen it all, including the slap and the broken shoe, lingering by the gates in order to enjoy the scene but too far distant to hear what had passed between the RSO and Tiffany Kane— they had slipped into the big house just before her and fled to their rooms, agog with excitement and the desire to spread the news that an affair was in being between the handsome surgeon and Tiffany and that there had been a lovers' quarrel in full view of anyone who happened to be passing.

Tiffany made her way to the ward and began the day's work with so little energy or enthusiasm that both Sister and Staff Nurse made a point of asking her if she was well. She could scarcely explain that she was afflicted with the disease for which there was no cure despite the claim of cynics that marriage was a certain cure for love. She would never have the opportunity to discover if there was any truth in the claim, she thought unhappily, as she assured her seniors that she was quite well and went on with her assigned tasks.

As the morning wore on, she began to feel

physically sick with apprehension at the thought of seeing Howard walk into the ward. She dreaded even the merest contact with him . . . at the same time, she hungered for a glimpse of him and allowed herself to indulge in a moment of wild fantasy in which they had never been at loggerheads, there was a mutual liking and attraction between them and he would instinctively look for her the moment he entered the ward and smile at her with a warmth and a secret intimacy which would give a radiance to the day and bring a leaping joy to her heart.

How would she face him—if she were called upon to do so? How could they meet, even in such ascetic and aseptic surroundings, without recalling their quarrel and the acrimony and violence and hatred which had existed between them? How could they speak to each other, if it proved necessary, with any degree of equanimity or ordinary civility?

And how could she risk meeting his eyes, even though they were cold and hostile and contemptuous, with the knowledge of her love for him so fierce and tumultuous within her breast? Would it be possible to school her expression, her eyes, her tone of voice so that he could not suspect the way she felt about him—when she longed to run to him, throw her arms about him, beg his forgiveness, plead for his respect if nothing else and search his proud, handsome face for the merest vestige of a smile, a relenting, a regret for all he had said and done to hurt and humiliate her?

She was on her way to the sluice with a covered receiver when the doors were opened abruptly and he strode into the ward . . . he checked his pace as they almost collided. For a long, tense moment they looked at each other—and then he stepped to one side without a word and she passed him as though he were a stranger while he looked over her head in search of Sister Adeline.

Tiffany bolted into the sluice, relinquished the receiver and buried her face in her hands while the hot, salt tears trickled through her shaking fingers. Not a word—not a smile—not the merest acknowledgment of her existence! But what had she expected, after all—was it likely that he would do anything but ignore her completely?

She had not known that love would be like this—so tempestuous, so demanding, so *hurtful*! And it would not have been if she had not been so stupid and reckless and mad! Why, oh why couldn't she have fallen in love with Michael who would cut off his right hand rather than hurt her in any way?

'Tiffany! My dear child! What on earth is wrong?' Sister Adeline hurried into the sluice, closing the door firmly behind her. The words were automatic . . . she knew perfectly well the explanation for these tears for it was all over the hospital that the RSO had been enjoying an affair with Tiffany and that they had quarrelled bitterly on the previous night. Paula had found herself scarcely able to answer the RSO's professional query and direct him to the bed of the patient he had come to see . . . and she had immediately gone in search of

Tiffany, having observed with some grimness the encounter at the door of the ward. She had known by the sudden tautness of his jaw that Howard Duffy had taken exception to her brisk, abrupt manner—but Paula had grown very fond of the little, warm-hearted, conscientious junior and, despite her own penchant for the RSO, she had felt immediate indignation when she learned that not only had he quarrelled violently with Tiffany but had also forgot himself to the point of physical abuse.

Tiffany Kane was popular with almost everyone . . . the RSO, despite his brilliance as a surgeon and the occasional warmth of manner which could charm so easily, would not have many supporters this day for there were few people who had not suffered at one time or another from his caustic tongue and abrupt arrogance and impatient demands. Because his work and his patients were always his first concern and he would allow nothing to affect either adversely, he had always been forgiven and the incident forgotten . . . but it was one thing to lash out at a colleague or a nurse with his tongue and quite another to use his hands to lash out at a girl he had been dating merely because she had angered him in some way or other.

Tiffany forced back her tears, hastily brushed her wet cheeks and bent low over the sink with the receiver she had hurriedly taken up.

'I'm all right, thank you, Sister,' she said stiffly, her throat aching with the effort to hold back the tears.

'Nonsense! You're not one to cry easily .. now come along! You can talk to me, you know.' And Paula turned the girl towards her and smiled down at that pale, tear-stained, distressed face.

'Really, Sister . . . it's nothing I can talk about to anyone,' Tiffany said as firmly as she could. 'It's a personal matter . . . something I must sort out for myself.'

Paula felt a warm compassion for this young, lovable girl. 'Do you care so much for him, Tiffany?' she asked gently. 'He doesn't seem to be worth it—I'd never trust myself to a man who can lose his temper to that extent.'

Tiffany stared at her in horror. Where she had been white she was ashen, her eyes enormous in her small, stricken face. Sister Adeline's words left her in no doubt whatsoever that she—and perhaps everyone else—knew exactly what had taken place between her and Howard Duffy.

'How do you know?' She could scarcely find her voice.

'My dear, it's all over the hospital,' Paula said quietly, regretfully.

'No . . . oh no! It can't be! He'll blame *me* . . . he'll hate me now if he never did before! Oh, Sister, what am I going to do?'

Paula cast an anxious glance towards the door as Tiffany's voice rose in a wail of despair. 'Do? Why, go off duty immediately, of course,' she said briskly. 'I can't have you on my ward in this state—and you're obviously not well enough to be on duty. I don't suppose you slept very much last night,' she added kindly.

'Run away, you mean?' Tiffany demanded. 'I'm not going to do that, Sister!' Her chin tilted with proud defiance. 'I'm quite capable of doing my work—and I promise you that there won't be any more tears. I feel much better now.' She smiled shakily. 'I think I needed to get it off my chest.'

'Was it just a silly tiff—or something more serious?' Paula asked, unable to resist the urging of a natural curiosity.

Tiffany hesitated, wondering exactly what was being said about her and the RSO 'all over the hospital.' The last thing she wanted was that he should receive the blame for their quarrel . . . why, even Sister Adeline who had always had a soft spot for Howard Duffy had spoken of him quite contemptuously and Tiffany shuddered to think what might be said and thought by those who did not like him very much.

'It was my fault,' she said quietly. 'Entirely my fault . . . I said some unforgivable things.' Remarks that she could not forgive herself, she thought sadly—words that must have convinced him that she was not only a flirt but entirely without morals . . .

CHAPTER TWELVE

TIFFANY scarcely knew how she struggled through the rest of the morning. She shrank from the unspoken sympathy of her fellow-nurses—and even a few of the patients who seemed to have heard the gossip which was being whispered so avidly in wards and corridors and departments all over St Christopher's. It must be a long time since the gossips had been offered anything so juicy, she thought bitterly—and wondered if Howard had realised that their quarrel was public knowledge or if he was going about his work in blessed ignorance.

She was free for a few hours that afternoon—and she knew that she could not remain anywhere in or near the hospital. She needed to get right away from Kit's for a little while—and she decided that she would visit her godmother. Rebecca would know nothing of this wretched business . . . she would greet her warmly and kindly, ply her with tea and cakes and, as always, avoid all mention of Kit's. Perhaps Tiffany would be able to forget her unhappiness and heartache and the very existence of Howard Duffy for a brief period of time . . .

She was crossing the Main Hall when she heard her name. She turned, recognising Michael's voice, barely able to muster a smile, so low were her spirits—and then she realised that he, too, had heard the gossip. Her heart sank . . . here was another man in her life who was facing her with anger in his eyes—and she wished devoutly, not for the first time, that she had followed the dictates of good sense and the advice of Jess Lomax and broken completely with Michael some time before. She had been seeing much less of him of late, hoping that he would realise the tepidity of her feelings and seek the company of other girls without forcing her to be brutally frank with him.

'Can you spare a minute, Tiffany?' he asked, looking down at her coldly.

'Of course . . . I'm just going off for a few hours,' she told him, as lightly as she could, a little dismayed by the hard, unfriendly look in his eyes.

'Then perhaps you'll have coffee with me at Benny's?' he suggested, taking her arm and guiding her towards the heavy glass doors which swung open automatically at their approach.

He did not speak as they walked down the gentle slope to the pavement, covered the few yards to the little side-street and crossed the road to Benny's Café, a popular haunt with the hospital staff.

He walked briskly, his relentless hand at her elbow and Tiffany had to hasten to keep up with him. She glanced up at his unusually stern face and although she could sympathise with his feelings she was a little cross with him at the same time. She understood that the gossip would affect him more than anyone but herself and Howard for their friendship was common knowledge and no doubt it was generally expected that it would eventually lead to marriage. The startling revelation, false though it was, that she had been having an affair with the RSO would have meant embarrassment and humiliation for Michael—he had no reason to doubt the truth of the gossip and probably her recent excuses for not accepting his invitations had suddenly assumed suspicious importance in his mind. She was cross with him for allowing everyone to imagine that an engagement between them was in the offing—and for believing the talk about her and Howard Duffy, as he so obviously had. He of all people should know her better, she thought indignantly . . .

Benny's was very busy at this time of the day but the timely exit of a young couple provided them with a small table in a fairly secluded corner—and Tiffany felt that its position would suit them very well if an argument was about to develop which seemed very likely for she was in no mood to be cross-examined by Michael about the truth or falsity of the current grapevine gossip.

He brought the coffees and sat down, facing her but without meeting her eyes. He spooned sugar into his coffee and sat stirring it thoughtfully while Tiffany tapped her fingers impatiently on the table top. At last, she could not stand his continued silence a moment longer.

'For heaven's sake!' she exploded. 'Say what you want to say and get it off your chest, Michael.'

He looked at her reproachfully. 'I suppose you know that people are talking about you and Duffy.'

Tiffany shrugged. 'Let them talk,' she retorted

defiantly, feeling that she was fast losing patience with all those people who had nothing better to do than repeat silly rumours.

'You might have been honest with me, Tiff,' he said abruptly, resentfully.

She sat back and looked at him squarely. 'And you think I haven't been?'

He gestured impatiently. 'Well, it's obvious, isn't it? I guessed you were getting tired of me but I didn't think you'd run around with another man behind my back. It seems so unlike you, Tiffany.'

'Perhaps because it isn't true,' she said coldly.

He smiled faintly, sadly. 'Why deny it? Don't I deserve the truth . . . we've been friends for a long time, you've meant a lot to me and I thought you were reasonably fond of me.'

Colour leaped to her face. It was a flush of annoyance at his readiness to believe the gossip rather than her denial . . . but Michael immediately construed it as a flooding of guilt.

'Oh, I don't mean to reproach you,' he said quietly. 'No doubt you had your reasons—I'm not a particularly exciting person and I would never expect to compete with Duffy. But then, I never thought such a situation would arise . . . for one thing, he's never taken much interest in any of Kit's staff in the past and for another thing I wouldn't have imagined that he might appeal to *you* at all. I suppose senior surgeons have a glamour that a mere medical student lacks—and so many girls seem to fall over themselves to attract Duffy. I just thought you were different, that's all.'

'And it doesn't occur to you that you might be right—that everyone else is wrong?' she asked drily.

'Oh, come, Tiff! You were seen quarrelling with him last night.'

'We've never been the best of friends, you know!' she retorted. 'Anyone who can believe the talk after the way he's been treating me for weeks must be completely mad!'

He looked at her sceptically. 'That's easily explained . . . merely an attempt to throw dust in everyone's eyes. After all, we all know that the authorities are not keen on affairs between senior and junior members of the staff.'

Tiffany sighed. 'It's hopeless,' she said wearily. 'Whatever I say you'll have an alternative explanation. I agree that the whole thing can be construed in two ways. But your way is the wrong way, Michael.'

He leaned forward and said quietly, almost beseechingly: 'Can you honestly tell me that Duffy doesn't mean a thing to you, Tiff?'

She was silent. If only he had phrased his question differently . . . if only he had not asked her so directly about her feelings for Howard.

He sat back abruptly. 'I see,' he said—and he was cold and unfriendly once more.

'You don't see at all,' she said bitterly.

Her tone struck him forcibly. He said evenly: 'I see that you know as well as I do that you're wasting your time, Tiff—he isn't a marrying man and you weren't any more than a casual affair.'

'There was never any affair, Michael,' she said dully, having reached the point where she no longer cared what he or anyone else thought.

'What's the use of hiding behind your pride? The whole hospital knows different,' he said crossly.

'Then perhaps someone should try asking Howard Duffy his opinion of me—and prepare for a shock!' she flared.

'You're just smarting from the things he said to you last night,' Michael said wisely.

'Someone was recording our conversation no doubt!' she snapped.

'Oh, I don't know what passed between you . . . you don't imagine I was interested in the details, do you?' His anger was stirring again as he remembered the sly amusement in the eyes of his colleague who had so obligingly supplied him with the facts about Tiffany and the RSO. 'Just have some thought for my feelings, that's all I ask! You're supposed to be my girl . . . I'd even contemplated asking you to marry me when I'd qualified and you'd finished your training,' he threw at her grimly.

'That would have been a mistake.'

'Obviously!'

'Oh, not in the way you mean. I've always been fond of you, Michael—but I would never have fallen in love with you or wanted to marry you.'

'You prefer to make a fool of yourself over a man who wouldn't have the decency to ask you to marry him!'

'It isn't a question of decency,' she retorted

bitingly. 'I shouldn't be at all surprised if Howard Duffy is thinking of me right now with loathing and contempt.'

'What happened? Did you lie to him too in order to meet another man? Did you lead him up the garden path too? I don't know what's got into you, Tiff—you never used to be that kind of girl! Unless Duffy isn't the first man you've been meeting behind my back!'

'I don't belong to you!' she snapped angrily.

'You were *my* girl,' he repeated stubbornly, sullenly.

'The past tense is particularly appropriate in the circumstances!'

'I entirely agree.' They were both angry now, glaring at each other across the table, the untouched coffees completely forgotten.

Tiffany rose abruptly. 'I have to go,' she announced.

'And I'm supposed to be in Casualty.' He rose almost at the same time.

'Well, Michael,' she said coldly. 'It's been nice knowing you.'

'It was a pity you had to ruin everything—including my memories of the good times we've had in the past,' he said, just as coldly. 'Now I shall never know if you're just a two-timing little flirt—or if you were once the sweet girl I liked so much and changed since you took up with Duffy.'

'I don't suppose you'll lose any sleep over the problem,' she assured him drily. 'I've never been so important in your life as you've liked to believe.'

She nodded to him curtly and walked towards the door of the café, ignoring the curious glances that followed her, aware that everyone in the place had listened with great interest to their last exchange of remarks for neither had bothered to lower their voices, so angry with each other had they felt.

Despite his claim that he was needed on Casualty, Michael sat down abruptly in his chair and glared at the occupants of the nearest tables who hastily resumed their interrupted conversation.

It was true enough that he had never been in love with Tiffany but nevertheless it was a blow to a man's pride to learn that she had been deliberately evading his company in order to go out with another man. Not content with that, she had to publicise her personal affairs to the point that everyone at Kit's was talking about her—and probably sniggering about his confident possessiveness of the past where Tiffany was concerned. Everyone knew that he had dated her regularly for well over a year . . . he had never denied the possibility that they would marry in time—and it had frequently occurred to him that he could do worse than to marry a girl who understood him and suited him so well.

Perhaps he had been a little too confident, a little too cocksure. Perhaps he had taken her affection for granted. Certainly he had contentedly believed that she cared for him enough to marry him when circumstances and finances would permit. He supposed it was mere sentiment that made him so angry with her, so despondent at the thought of her treachery, so conscious that the lack of her company and affection would create a void that might prove difficult to fill. And perhaps it was a flicker of natural resentment that she had obviously not cared very much for him at all . . . a marked blow to his vanity. What did she want of a man, he wondered bitterly—he had always been courteous and considerate, sympathetic and understanding, gentle and affectionate and undemanding, allowing her to take the lead in their relationship and never forcing the pace—he was considered to be passably good-looking and intelligent and he prided himself on his even temper and eagerness to please . . . what on earth *did* she want of a man?

Whatever she sought, she had not found it in Howard Duffy, by all accounts, he thought with a surge of petty delight in her discomfiture. He was a man who did not hesitate to show rudeness and inconsideration, could scarcely be called sympathetic—and, if rumour was to be believed in full, did not even hesitate to resort to violence when a woman failed to live up to his expectations. Well, the affair was at an end now—and perhaps Tiffany had learned her lesson. She had not only quarrelled with Duffy but she had also lost a much more worthwhile claimant for her affections, he told himself with some degree of complacency.

As for himself . . . well, there were other women in the world and Tiffany had not really been so exceptional. Pretty, yes . . . but somewhat naïve and immature. Sweet, yes . . . but how much of her sweetness was ingrained and how much an adopted pose was something that he would never be able to determine now. If it were not for the humiliation she had brought upon him by her deceit and deception, he could have dismissed her from his life and his affections with only a faint regret and a nostalgia for the good times they had known together. As it was, they had parted on bad terms and he felt that he could never again think of her without anger and animosity . . .

Rebecca gave her god-daughter a warm, surprised welcome when she arrived so unexpectedly at her house. 'Why didn't you let me know you were coming?' she reproached lightly. 'I have to take tea with my publisher at four—and I don't think I can break the appointment at this late hour.'

'I can't stay long,' Tiffany assured her, sinking into a deep armchair with a faint sigh. 'I'm due to go back on duty at four, anyway.'

Rebecca glanced at the clock. 'You've come a long way for a short stay,' she said curiously. She looked more closely at the girl's white, strained features and the unusual slumping of her slim shoulders. 'What's wrong, darling?' she asked gently, picking up a magazine and leafing idly through its pages.

'Oh, I don't know . . . everything—nothing!' She mustered a bleak smile. 'I didn't come to burden you with my troubles, Rebecca—I just wanted to escape for a few hours.'

'That's just as well,' Rebecca retorted briskly.

'This is a new dress and I simply can't allow you to weep all over it.'

Tiffany's smile deepened just a fraction. 'I've never been the weeping kind.'

'Until now,' Rebecca said shrewdly. 'You'd better tell me all about it . . . as briefly as possible.' Although she spoke so lightly, with so much apparent unconcern, her words and tone were no guide to her very real anxiety and apprehension.

Tiffany could not have borne sympathy and urgent appeals to unburden herself . . . Rebecca's blunt and direct approach was just what she needed. She told the story quietly and without emotion, neither asking nor expecting sympathy or support.

'Silly girl!' Rebecca exclaimed, having heard her out in silence. 'Now what are you going to do?'

Tiffany shrugged. 'Bear with the talk until it dies down, I suppose . . . it will only be a nine days' wonder. And avoid Howard Duffy as much as possible.' She had given the bare facts briefly and concisely, without making any mention of her unsuspected and so newly-discovered love for Howard or her recent quarrel with Michael Gilroy.

'I can't blame him for being cross with you,' Rebecca said unexpectedly. 'What on earth possessed you to accept invitations from Justin Amery, in the first place?'

'I like him!' Tiffany said defiantly.

'No doubt you do—but you could have met him often enough in this house without indulging in clandestine meetings.'

'There was nothing clandestine about them!' protested Tiffany, hurt. 'His wife knew he was seeing me!'

'Do you imagine the world would believe that? And Howard Duffy is a very worldly man, my dear. I must thank him for trying to protect you from your own naïvety, Tiffany.'

Her god-daughter stared at her in astonishment. 'You really mean that, don't you?' she asked blankly.

'Of course. Oh, I shall be quite diplomatic, don't worry—I won't let him know that you've told me anything about your stupid difference of opinion.'

'He hit me!' Tiffany exclaimed indignantly.

'And so would I smack a child for playing with fire,' Rebecca said, smiling. 'You're a sensible girl when you choose to be, my dear . . . you know perfectly well that a concerned and anxious parent often smacks a child who has just been dragged back from disaster—it's a very human reaction.'

'You don't imagine that Howard felt any paternal concern for me, do you?' Tiffany said scornfully.

Rebecca resumed her careless skimming of her magazine. 'He's old enough to feel paternal about a young girl, isn't he?' she asked casually.

'For heaven's sake, Rebecca . . . he's only in his early thirties!'

Rebecca hastily hid a smile. She had come to know Tiffany very well . . . and she had not been slow to understand all that she had omitted from her story. The girl's instinctive indignation at the thought of the handsome young surgeon taking only a paternal interest in her had confirmed Rebecca's vague suspicion . . . and now she was curious to find out for herself how Howard Duffy really felt about Tiffany. For it was certainly not acceptable to a woman who knew her world and her fellow beings that any man could become so violently angry in such circumstances unless there was a certain jealousy in his heart and mind . . . although he might very well be ignorant of the fact or chary of giving the emotion its right name.

She had taken a warm liking to the young surgeon—and she had followed her liking with the offer of her friendship. But Rebecca did not think that there was much love on his side in that affair— and it would not be surprising if a man's taste, jaded by the selfish sophistication and vain affections of a woman like Shona Sinclair, turned abruptly towards the sweet, unspoiled nature of a Tiffany Kane.

And Tiffany? Well, it would not be surprising if her youthful, untouched heart had responded to a warm and vital magnetism in the man that even Rebecca had sensed and appreciated.

CHAPTER THIRTEEN

Howard knew and detested the rumours that were circulating . . . and he could scarcely be civil or patient with anyone, so furious was he with a stupid, talkative, vindictive girl who could not keep a still tongue in her head where her affairs were concerned.

He was very confident that no one would dare approach him for confirmation or denial of the gossip—and, indeed, he barely gave anyone the opportunity, going about his work with a cold, forbidding expression in his eyes and cutting conversation to the barest minimum.

He realised perfectly well that he was not only on trial but had also been condemned by his colleagues and juniors—it was obvious by the swift, wary glances that the young nurses flashed at him in passing and the stiff disapproval he sensed in people who had always treated him with a degree of warmth and affability. His shoulders were broad, he thought contemptuously—this would die a sudden death when something else came along to divert the gossips. In a month, perhaps less, it would be completely forgotten.

But he was amazed to realise how many people believed him capable of an affair with a junior nurse when he had always taken pains to avoid becoming personally involved with any member of the staff. How willing, how delighted they all were to be given the opportunity to think ill of him!

Let them think—let them talk, he said to himself, unconsciously adopting Tiffany's own attitude. He would not allow himself to dwell on the events of that night—certainly had neither wish nor intent to think of the girl in question. It had been absolute folly to concern himself with her affairs . . . this was what came of allowing his innate interest and compassion for his fellow-beings to over-ride common sense and discretion! It should not matter to him if a young girl ruined her reputation and lost her job because of a silly infatuation for a married man . . . it did not matter to him, he reminded himself firmly.

His interference—and he admitted that it had been unwarranted and deservedly unwelcome—had nothing to do with the fact that Tiffany Kane was young and pretty and appealingly naïve, he thought resolutely, almost sternly. He would have reacted in almost exactly the same way to the discovery that any girl was on the brink of ruining her life—be she as plain as a pikestaff!

It was only because he sensed that the young nurse was innocent and inexperienced that he had been so appalled to learn that she was carrying on an affair with Justin Amery. However innocuous it might have been so far, she certainly had accepted an invitation to spend a weekend with the man—and she could not be so naïve as to be ignorant of his expectations! He was angry and contemptuous at the thought of Amery . . . but at the same time he appreciated that Tiffany could have a strong appeal to any man and, if she had seemed willing and infatuated as he did not doubt she had, then perhaps Amery was not entirely to blame for crediting her with past affairs. Her very innocence and naïvety were her worst enemies, he thought ruefully—although it was true that they should protect her from the advances of any man. Amery must be infatuated, too—too obsessed with her youthful sweetness and prettiness and appealing ways to realise her obvious inexperience.

She should have more sense! He was surprised that no one else had thought to warn her that her eager friendliness and light-hearted, coquettish approach could so easily be misconstrued by men. And she claimed to be rising twenty-three . . . he was amazed that she had never before suffered at the hands of some unscrupulous man!

He had misconstrued her friendliness himself, he recalled abruptly—and wondered when he had come to realise that he had been misjudging her for weeks. The girl was a virtual stranger—and yet he was finding excuses for her behaviour with absolute confidence in his verdict on her true nature. When had it occurred to him that she did not mean to flirt with every man who came in her way? When had it dawned on him that she was innately innocent, certainly untouched and virtually unawakened, that she was refreshingly young and naïve and completely lacking in the sophistication and affectation which marked so many girls of her age?

And what the devil possessed him that he could not put the girl out of his mind? She had no liking or respect for him . . . she was certainly not allowing thoughts of him to intrude into her work . . . or if she did think of him during the days that followed that ridiculous quarrel then it was only with anger and contempt and hatred for the humiliation he had heaped on her and his impertinence in trying to run her life. He simply could not understand why he should retreat from the thought of her dislike and animosity . . . after all, he had known before they quarrelled that she disliked him—and certainly he had given her ample cause to do so. What on earth was he about to feel a foolish, unwelcome, sentimental regret for the disappointing pattern that their association had followed since that very first day—and why, in heaven's name, should he think of it as disappointing?!

If he were less adult, less experienced, he might believe that he was falling in love with Tiffany Kane, he told himself grimly. But he was adult and experienced! Was he so sure that he was being absolutely honest with himself . . . ?

When he read Rebecca Waring's letter, inviting him to a small dinner-party, he was in two minds as to his acceptance. Although he had never been particularly conscious of it in the past, for some reason it occurred to him immediately that the novelist was godmother to Tiffany—and it might be that she had heard of his contretemps with her god-daughter and wished to talk to him about it. Yet would she have sent such a warm and friendly letter of invitation if she was displeased or angry with him? Would she have bothered to invite him to her house at all in the circumstances? No, it was unlikely that Tiffany had mentioned that matter to her . . . he had certainly gained the impression that the girl did not live in her godmother's pocket and he had dined at the house several times without hearing any mention of her.

He wondered why Tiffany had mentioned their quarrel at all to anyone—as she must have done for it to become so widely known to all at Kit's. She had been upset, angry . . . perhaps she had blurted it out impulsively to a sympathetic friend at the time and regretted it later, he thought charitably, realising abruptly that he was again seeking to find excuses for a girl who seemed to be attaining a certain, odd, almost unwelcome importance in his thoughts and feelings . . .

He liked and admired Rebecca Waring—had very much appreciated her wit and intelligence and vivacity, the odd, amusing affectations, the bluntness of her remarks and the impish sense of humour. Why should he withdraw from a friendship that he enjoyed simply because she chanced to be connected with Tiffany Kane? He decided to accept the invitation . . . and sat down immediately at his desk to write his acceptance.

Rebecca read the brief, friendly note and smiled to herself with satisfaction. She had feared that he might refuse because of her link with Tiffany, because they had met in her house for the first time, socially, because there was always the risk that he might meet her again under her godmother's roof. She was pleased that his affection for her had withstood these dangers—and even more convinced that he was exactly the man to take care of the inexperienced, foolish, reckless Tiffany with her ignorance of the dangers that lay in wait for girls with her particular brand of sweetness and a touching but treacherous faith in human nature.

Rebecca sat back and took a cigarette from the box on her bureau, inserted it carefully into her long holder and reached for a table lighter. She had done her part, she thought complacently . . . now it was up to them to settle their differences like responsible and adult human beings . . . and heaven help them both if they dared to carry on their quarrel beneath her roof!

It had been decided for some time that Tiffany would arrange to be free to dine with Rebecca and a few friends on her birthday. But she had impressed upon her godmother that she had no heart for a big party and Rebecca had assured her that she would invite only a few of Tiffany's favourite people.

Everything seemed to conspire to make her late for the engagement. She was due to go off duty at five but a rush of emergency admissions, due to the collision of a bus with a petrol tanker, kept everyone on their toes that afternoon and it was almost six before Tiffany was sent off the ward with a grateful word of thanks from the harassed Sister Adeline.

When she reached the Nurses' Home, having hurried across the park in a torrent of driving rain, she felt tired and a little depressed and in no mood to go out again on such a terrible night.

But she could not disappoint Rebecca. So she hastily slipped out of her uniform and into her dressing-gown and went to have a quick bath, hoping that it would refresh her. Jess came out of the bathroom as she approached, similarly clad in dressing-gown and slippers and carrying her towel.

'There isn't any hot water, Tiffany,' she said quietly.

Tiffany paused in dismay. 'Oh no!'

As though she sensed reproach, Jess said quickly: 'Don't blame me—I'm disappointed too! There must be something wrong with the system.'

Winnie, the little maid, came bustling down the corridor at that moment. 'There's no hot water, nurses,' she said to them in passing. 'You'll have to take a cold shower and like it!'

Tiffany grimaced at the woman's back for Winnie was not very popular with any of the girls, being too prone to grumble and too quick to imagine offence where none existed if they tried to tease her out of her usual irritability.

'Do you want to use the shower? Are you going out? I'm not in a hurry,' Jess said obligingly.

'I'm dining with Rebecca—oh, I shall have to do without a shower. I really haven't time, anyway. I'm late as it is.'

Jess walked beside her to the door of her room. 'You must have been busy on Adeline today,' she said, her tone faintly implying that she was only making conversation.

'Yes we were.' Tiffany opened her door.

'By the way . . . I haven't wished you a happy birthday,' Jess blurted, colouring.

Tiffany smiled. 'It's a bit late in the day—but thanks.'

'I haven't seen you until now,' Jess pointed out.

'Oh, I wasn't reproaching you,' Tiffany said quickly. 'Look, I must get ready, Jess—I'll see you some time tomorrow.'

Once in her room, with her door closed, Tiffany sighed. Even Jess had turned against her, she thought bitterly—for the first surge of sympathy for the junior nurse, so popular and personable, had abruptly veered towards the RSO. He must have had his reasons for breaking with her so violently, the gossips argued—he must have been hard-pressed to lose his temper so completely. She had herself to blame for taking up with someone so much senior in the first place—and why should she have encouraged his attentions when she had a perfectly good boy-friend in Michael Gilroy? Now she had lost both the RSO and the medical student—and perhaps she would think twice before she played fast and loose with any man's affections in the future! For it was generally assumed that as Tiffany Kane had been capable of deceiving Michael Gilroy about her association with the RSO, then she might have been equally capable of deceiving the RSO where another man was concerned. Hadn't she always been attractive and responsive to men? Hadn't she always seemed something of a flirt despite her apparent loyalty to Michael Gilroy?

Tiffany was not insensitive to the sudden change of feeling . . . and she was no longer so naïve and trusting as she had been. She realised perfectly well that Howard Duffy's physical attractions combined with a little jealousy of her supposed success where others had failed made it easy for her fellow-nurses to find excuses for him and blame for her . . . but she was past caring what any of them thought. She had found it useless to deny the rumours—and her stubborn silence even in the face of questions from her close friends made it difficult for them to believe her innocent of the accusations.

Jess had scoffed at the idea that Tiffany could have had an affair with the RSO. She had stoutly defended Tiffany and spoken to her friend at the first opportunity to discover how she felt about the foolish and certainly baseless rumours. It had been rather unfortunate that Tiffany was at the end of her tether after a trying and miserable day. She had snapped at her friend irritably, refusing to discuss the matter, and accused poor Jess of being as ready to believe the worst of her as everyone else. It was not surprising that Jess should be deeply hurt—or that she should immediately suppose that there must be some truth in the talk or Tiffany would have laughed with her at the extravagant claims of the gossips.

They had parted with a decided coolness between them . . . and later, Jess learning of her break with Michael and convinced that he must be hurt and disappointed by Tiffany's odd behaviour, she had also been angry with the girl and felt that she would not readily forgive her for treating Michael so casually and cruelly when he had always been such a good friend.

They had avoided each other as much as possible—and Jess's transference to night duty had made it easier than in normal circumstances. Tiffany missed the warm affection and companionship of her friend—but she felt that it was merely one more straw to add to the load she carried on her heart.

She was beginning to feel that she could not go on with her training. The censure and disapproval that she sensed on all sides, the knowledge that Howard thought her so completely beneath his notice that he deliberately looked the other way if they chanced to pass in a corridor or on the ward and the agonising burden of her love for him were all becoming too much for her. She longed for her home and family, familiar surroundings and complete forgetfulness of Kit's and all it had stood for in her life—and never more so than on this day, her birthday. Tiffany had always been rather sentimental about birthdays—she was deeply pained and regretful that this particular anniversary of her birth should have been accompanied by so much heartache and unhappiness.

But she had the evening with Rebecca, she reminded herself, resolving to enjoy it as much as she could in the circumstances. After all, this was not the end of the world—there were other careers if she decided to leave nursing—and she supposed there were other men, even one man who might be able to eradicate the image of Howard in her heart and mind and make it possible for her to be happy and eager and light-hearted once again . . .

The house was blazing with light as she paid off the taxi and hurried towards the main door. For no known reason, she was reminded rather poignantly of another night when she had arrived at Rebecca's house to find it warm and welcoming with its lighted windows . . . the night when she had met Justin for the first time and surprisingly met Howard Duffy and, she supposed sadly, fallen in love with him quite against her will. She recalled her dislike of his fiancée—and wondered if that had stemmed from jealousy. She supposed that he was still engaged to the glamorous film star—and it did not help to remember that Justin had assured her that to his knowledge no engagement existed between them. She would never know the truth now, she thought bitterly—unless she read about it in the newspapers . . . and when she was back at her home in Somerset and surrounded with the love and affection and reassurance of her family and friends, it might not mean very much to her that Howard Duffy was going to marry another woman. She could hope, she told herself defiantly—knowing that it was not a hope at all but something she dreaded instinctively.

Jeeves admitted her to the house with a smile of welcome . . . inasmuch as he ever allowed himself to smile upon anyone. Tiffany slipped up to her usual room to leave her things before entering the

TREAD SOFTLY, NURSE 171

lounge. The hum of voices and the chink of glasses warned her that the other guests were already in evidence and enjoying cocktails before dinner.

She wore a simple, black dress, high-heeled black shoes and pearls in her ears and about her throat to relieve her sombre appearance. She had intended, if there had been time, to pile her red hair high on her head in a mass of curls and caught up with a matching black ribbon . . . instead she had left it in its usual neat roll and she felt that it did not really matter. She did not feel particularly festive . . . she would have preferred a quiet evening on her own to hug her unhappiness to her breast and mourn all that she had lost or never known . . .

The room quietened as she opened the door and paused on the threshold. Tiffany glanced about her, smiling, faint colour in her cheeks and a warmth stealing into her heart as she recognised that Rebecca had kept her word—it was a small party, made up of people that she particularly liked and admired . . . and then she met the startled, angry eyes of a man across the room and every vestige of colour fled from her face.

She would have bolted from the room in that moment if Rebecca had not taken her firmly by the arm and drawn her into the group . . .

To safeguard her plans, Rebecca had told none of her guests that she was expecting Tiffany that night—and Howard was both astonished and very angry when she walked into the room.

For two pins, he would have walked out of the house, he assured himself fiercely—and knew that, while he might have a reputation for rudeness, he could neither offend the charming and likeable Rebecca Waring nor humiliate the little nurse so publicly.

He stood apart while the others surrounded Tiffany with warm welcomes and wishes—for Rebecca had immediately announced her as the guest of honour and explained that it was her birthday. Howard watched the group coldly, wondering how he could be expected to talk to Tiffany Kane with any degree of amiability, how he could be pleasant to her at all—when his only impulse, so strong that it dismayed him, was to take her by the arm and lead her off to a quiet corner and demand what the devil she meant by intruding so much into his thoughts and emotions of late!

CHAPTER FOURTEEN

TIFFANY smiled and responded to the greetings and good wishes with automatic warmth, her heart pounding and the ice of apprehension stealing over her entire body.

This was Rebecca's doing, she thought angrily—how could she have invited Howard to Tiffany's birthday dinner when she knew, better than most, exactly how she felt about him and what had so recently passed between them? Did she imagine that they would kiss and make up beneath her roof? Didn't she realise how much Tiffany loathed and despised the man—or how much he detested her in return, she demanded silently, furiously denying that such a description of her feelings where he was concerned was utterly false!

Love him! How could she love him—when he stood to one side, so arrogant, so cold, so indifferent, so cruel, making a pointed and humiliating display of his lack of interest in the guest of honour that Rebecca was so warmly acclaiming.

Rebecca ignored the reproach and accusation in Tiffany's eyes . . . she had not really expected any other reaction to the presence of Howard Duffy. And his air of indifference, the expression in *his* eyes, the stiff, uncompromising attitude of the man—this was exactly what she had hoped for it confirmed her very strong suspicion that he was not in the least indifferent to the youthful Tiffany. No matter what they might fear, she was quite certain that no one else in the room noticed their strange, mutual tension.

She drew the reluctant Tiffany towards Howard Duffy. 'And you know each other, of course,' she said lightly, carelessly.

Howard looked over her head: Tiffany did not dare to raise her eyes above his chin. 'Yes, of course,' Howard agreed stiffly.

'I forbid either of you to talk "shop" tonight,' Rebecca warned them gaily. 'I know what it is when two people in the same profession get together—but I'm sure you must have many other interests in common and this might be an excellent opportunity to discover them. Your glass is empty, Howard . . . have another cocktail. Tiffany only cares for fruit juice, by the way . . . you'll excuse me, won't you—I must find out why dinner is so delayed!'

Howard and Tiffany were left together—and each found it impossible to turn away when Rebecca had so obviously manoeuvred this proximity.

Tiffany began to tremble. She knew that someone had to break the silence before it became too painful . . . she realised only too well that he had no intention of doing so.

'This is nothing to do with me,' she said in a low, urgent voice. 'I didn't know you would be here tonight.'

'Or you wouldn't have come, presumably,' he

returned coldly, not quite sure if he believed her claim.

'Did you know that this dinner was planned as a birthday celebration for me?' she asked anxiously.

'No, I did not,' he replied vehemently.

'Or you wouldn't be here now,' she said, turning the tables.

'Probably not,' he admitted curtly. 'It seems you had the good sense not to advertise our quarrel outside the hospital, at least,' he added drily.

Tiffany looked up at him quickly . . . meeting his eyes for the first time. 'I didn't advertise it at all!' she said indignantly.

He smiled faintly, insolently. 'Do you expect me to believe you?'

'No . . . why should you? You're incapable of thinking any good of me at all,' she retorted. 'But it happens to be true, nevertheless . . . whatever story was circulated at Kit's, I assure you that I had nothing to do with it.'

'You seem to have played a very negative part altogether,' he said cynically. 'Except where Amery is concerned, perhaps.'

Her face flamed as she recalled the stupid, incriminating things she had said to him that night. 'You believed that, didn't you?' she said bitterly. 'No doubt you found it easy to believe . . . you never had anything good to say for me even before that particular night.' She turned away abruptly as Rebecca came back into the room and crossed to her side.

'Did you get your drink, darling?' Rebecca asked

lightly. Then, noticing that she carried no glass: 'Oh dear . . . and I thought I'd left you in Howard's capable hands!'

Her voice carried as it was meant to do . . . and he came forward swiftly, a rueful expression in his eyes. 'I'm afraid I forgot all about it, Rebecca . . . we were talking of other things.'

'I hope you complimented Tiffany on her appearance,' Rebecca said outrageously. 'I've never seen her look so pretty—and I'm not a susceptible male!'

Howard could have retorted that the girl seemed to have lost all her vivacious prettiness of late—and that he had been more conscious of that fact than he cared to admit even to himself.

Tiffany broke in hastily: 'Please, Rebecca! I'm sure Mr Duffy doesn't care to be forced into saying pretty things—and I really don't care to hear them. You know I dislike personal comments.'

'*Mr Duffy!* So formal!' Rebecca exclaimed in mock rebuke. 'Tiffany, you will make Howard feel like an unwanted guest if you treat him so coldly.'

'We've never been on first name terms,' Tiffany said, a little crossly. 'You seem to forget that I hold a very junior position at Kit's and that Mr Duffy is a senior surgeon.'

'I don't know anything about hospital etiquette and I really don't wish to know,' Rebecca retorted gaily. 'Under my roof, as fellow-guests, you are Howard and Tiffany to each other—or I shall be very displeased with both of you. Now, come along . . . dinner is about to be served. I've placed Howard on your right, child—so you must see to it that he enjoys his dinner. You may be the guest of honour but I expect you to help me in the role of hostess, you know!'

They walked across the hall to the spacious, elegant dining-room in complete silence while Rebecca busily gathered together the other guests and ushered them from the lounge.

Despite everything, Howard could not help being a little amused. Rebecca was so blatantly thrusting them together and he found himself wondering how much she really knew about their feelings for each other—and if she were determined, for reasons of her own, to bring about a reconciliation. She was undeniably fond of Tiffany and it must be obvious to anyone who knew affection for the girl that she was deeply unhappy. Why, even he was conscious of the misery lurking in the lovely eyes which had always held so much merriment and warmth and zest for life. Was it entirely his fault? he wondered with a faint pang of conscience. He knew how much she had suffered because of the gossip . . . so much of it recently having been unkind and distasteful. Where it had earned his contempt it was possible that Tiffany, more sensitive to public opinion, had been extremely hurt and upset.

He had been so convinced that she had betrayed their quarrel, however unintentionally—now he began to doubt his certainty. She had denied it—and there had been the ring of truth in her indignant protest. It was always possible that they had been seen or overheard, he admitted for the first time—and not really so unlikely, he thought ruefully, wishing that if they had been meant to quarrel they might have been blessed with greater privacy. Of course, he should not have lost his temper in the first place . . . and, equally of course, she had naturally resented his interference.

Such a stupid quarrel, he thought in retrospect. And wondered, as he settled himself in his place at the table, glancing briefly at her pale, troubled face, if she had spent that proposed weekend with Justin Amery. The very thought of Tiffany in the man's arms, accepting and responding to his embraces, filled him with a deep and frightening anger—and he had to hastily reassure himself that the innocence of her mind and heart was still evident in her eyes.

Tiffany met that quick, searching glance and wondered in her turn why he had turned to her so swiftly and unexpectedly. What were his thoughts? Was he as disconcerted and embarrassed by this second encounter beneath Rebecca's roof as she was? Did he really believe that she had engineered it when surely he must know that she wished as little personal contact with him as he obviously wanted with her?

It was true! she assured herself firmly as her heart instinctively protested the treachery of her thoughts. The notion that she was in love with him had been nothing more than a ridiculous fancy . . . well, she was cured now! No one could love a man who had treated her as Howard Duffy had during the past few weeks! Even now, fellow-guests through no fault of their own, he could not find the courtesy to talk to her, devoting himself almost entirely to Rebecca on his other side.

Rebecca reminded him in vain that he should be paying some attention to Tiffany . . . he seemed to choose just the moment when she was talking to someone else to turn towards her . . . and then, with a faint shrug of his shoulders implying that Tiffany evidently did not lack attention, he would turn back to Rebecca and resume their conversation. Fortunately the night was yet young . . . she would be disappointed indeed if nothing came of her plans before the evening ended. Not only disappointed but also extremely annoyed with the proud and difficult young man—any fool must be aware that Tiffany was painfully conscious of Howard Duffy and longing for some little warmth, some kindness, some hint of the olive branch where he was concerned . . .

It did not occur to Howard as they lingered over the meal and then returned to the lounge for easy, informal conversation, the steady flow of drinks, music for dancing supplied by the luxurious and expensive stereo system, that Tiffany was in the least conscious of him or waiting for him to make any move towards a better understanding between them. For she was apparently enjoying herself—and seemed to be deliberately avoiding his company and his conversation. He was a little bored, a little annoyed and a little too obvious in his attentions to the other women who were present.

Tiffany watched him while seemingly never once allowing her glance to turn in his direction. She felt sick at heart as she noticed the light banter which passed between him and Rachel Jefferson, the actress. Her chin tilted with faint, defiant contempt as he danced in easy, hurtful intimacy with Sonia Partridge, the novelist. She turned away with a swift pain at her heart as he looked, laughing, into the provocative eyes of Anna Madison, wife of an artist who was also present. Yet he ignored her, she thought resentfully. He did not cross the room to talk to her, to invite her to dance—his indifference to her was as marked here, in the company of those she thought her friends, people she liked and admired and who were kind and affectionate and sincere towards her, as at any time in the precincts of Kit's since they had met. And surely her friends, observant, thoughtful, kindly, were paying her even more attention than usual—not because it was her birthday or her party but because they recognised Howard's attitude and knew that she was so hurt by it. She could not bear any more of this public and painful humiliation . . . Abruptly, with a hasty word of excuse, she left Sean Madison with an unfinished remark on his lips and fled from the room via the windows to the terrace. She needed to be alone—and she needed the privacy and peace of the dark, moonless night to shed the tears which were already brimming on her lashes.

And Howard watched her go, scarcely attending to Rebecca who had joined him . . . wondering why Tiffany had rushed away so impulsively, wondering if he had only imagined that she was on the verge of tears, wondering if he would only invite anger and abuse if he followed her.

'. . . the weekend with the Amerys?' Rebecca trailed off, glancing up at him curiously.

Howard's attention was caught by the name. 'I'm sorry . . . what did you say?'

Rebecca sighed faintly. 'I merely asked you if you knew that Tiffany spent the weekend with the Amerys,' she repeated patiently.

'The Amerys?'

'Justin and Helen Amery,' she reminded him, a little puzzled by the sharpness of his tone. 'Tiffany has been very friendly with them both since she met Justin at one of my parties. They seem to have taken a liking for her . . . and apparently she is wonderful with their children.'

Howard stared down at her, frowning. It had never occurred to him that Tiffany might be friendly with both Justin *and* his wife . . . he had been so quick to assume that any friendship between the girl and the older man must be clandestine. And she had made no attempt to put him right! Any girl would have been indignant, even angry at such an interpretation to her friendship with any man . . . why had Tiffany allowed him to think evil of her in such a way? It was always possible that it was Rebecca who preferred to believe Tiffany's assurances that the association was perfectly innocent.

'I knew that she liked him,' he said slowly, cautiously.

'I think everyone must,' Rebecca replied lightly.

'Such a charming, courteous man—and so devoted to his wife and children. Tiffany has a great admiration for him.'

'Rather an odd friendship for a girl of Tiffany's age and interests, don't you think?' he asked quietly.

Rebecca chuckled. 'Oh, the world might imagine so . . . but we know Tiffany better, surely? She is rather naïvely liberal with her affections—but there isn't an ounce of silly sentiment in her make-up, thank heavens. Justin Amery is no more than a friend to Tiffany . . . she can never have enough friends, it seems—and that isn't such a bad policy in life. Far better than making enemies, don't you agree?' she added, a little slyly.

'Yes . . . life's too short for that kind of thing,' he agreed absently, his gaze on the long windows that dominated the room, his thoughts with the girl on the terrace rather than his hostess. He said abruptly: 'I seem to have had little opportunity to talk to Tiffany this evening . . . she has been so much in demand. But I think she's slipped out for a little air—and this might be a good moment to be sure of her attention for a few minutes. Would you excuse me, Rebecca?'

Rebecca beamed her approval. 'Of course—of course! No "shop" now!' she called after him as he strode purposefully across the room . . .

Tiffany stood against the stone balustrade, staring blindly into the darkness, the tears running unchecked down her face. She had never been so unhappy, so miserable . . . never been more conscious that she must get away from Kit's, from the gossip, from Howard Duffy. Her heart ached for the love and reassurance and comfort she must surely find with her family and her home . . .

Suddenly Howard was at her side and she caught the gleam of the white handkerchief he was holding out to her. 'Tears on your birthday,' he said gently. 'Do you want bad luck for the whole of the year?'

His voice was so soft, so kind, so unexpectedly sympathetic that the tears flowed even faster—and she snatched his handkerchief and turned away from him fiercely, mopping angrily at her wet cheeks.

He moved so that he faced her, took the handkerchief from her resisting fingers and completed the task of drying her tears. 'No more, please,' he begged lightly. 'I haven't an unlimited supply of hankies, you know.'

She smiled involuntarily . . . the merest glimmer of a smile that he was not even sure that it could be so described.

'I won't ask what's wrong,' he went on quietly. 'I think I know . . .'

'Don't leap to conclusions again,' she told him crossly, hating him for having found her in tears, hating him more because he had caused them with his cruel and unnecessary hostility.

He was silent for a moment, wondering how to reach her, knowing that he had behaved so badly that it was unlikely that she could ever forgive him, facing for the first time the unmistakable knowledge that he desired and needed not only her forgiveness but her love. For this young, foolish, innocent and appealing girl with the piquant face and shining red hair had carved a place for herself in his heart even while he had never believed that such a thing could happen. The intensity of his feelings, the desire to cherish and protect and surround her with constant happiness, astounded him—at the same time, it thrilled him because he had always doubted that he could give his heart so completely, so sincerely, so deeply. But there was no doubting the emotion that swept through him now as he looked down at her small, distressed face and longed to take her into his arms and kiss away every trace of her tears . . .

'Tiffany, there isn't much I can say—except that I'm sorry.' The words were low, urgent and holding more than a hint of appeal.

'Why should you be?' she demanded fiercely. 'I assure you that I'm not upset because of anything you've said or done, Mr Duffy.'

'*Mr Duffy!* So formal!' he said teasingly, echoing Rebecca's rebuking words.

'I may make silly mistakes—but I don't make them twice!' she retorted. 'It didn't take me long to learn that you don't welcome informality or anything else from a mere junior nurse.'

'We aren't on duty now, Tiffany,' he pointed out.

'Oh, does it make a difference?' she demanded drily.

He grinned suddenly. 'We weren't very formal with each other the last time we met outside a hospital ward.'

'I'm so pleased that the recollection amuses you!' she snapped.

He touched her cheek lightly, tenderly with his fingers. 'Poor Tiffany—I was an absolute brute to you that night. But you haven't been very kind to me—leaving me in suspense! I've been expecting to hear from your solicitors every morning, you know.'

'There was enough talk without going that far,' she said stiffly, a little embarrassed by the reminder of her impulsive and rather foolish threat.

'I really am sorry,' he said abruptly—and more convincingly than the gentle assurance had seemed to Tiffany. 'I had no right to interfere—then.'

She looked up at him quickly, her attention caught by the addition so quietly and meaningly spoken. 'Then?' she queried, unable to suppress her curiosity.

'I didn't know at that time that I loved you,' he told her quietly.

Her eyes widened and she gave a little gasp of astonishment. 'What did you say?' she demanded although she knew that she had heard him only too well. Her heart was threatening to break its bonds, so tumultuous was the storm of emotion which invaded it at his words—and her question came breathlessly.

'I love you, Tiffany—and I'm as surprised as you are. It seems so unlikely, doesn't it? It took me a long time to realise that I was so angry with you for meeting Amery because I was jealous. I suppose I didn't want to believe that I was capable of such a stupid and harmful emotion. But I was jealous—insanely so. I've been punishing you ever since—and myself, too. Things might have been so very different,' he added ruefully.

'I don't understand . . .' she faltered. 'How can you say that you love me!'

'I seem to have an amazing degree of courage,' he agreed lightly. 'After all, why should you even want to listen? Perhaps I should apologise for taking up your time with such foolishness—and make myself scarce.' He gave a heavy, mock sigh. 'People have always accused me of arrogance—and I seem to have made a habit of being presumptuous where you are concerned. How can I expect your friendship now—let alone your liking!'

Tiffany eyed him suspiciously. 'I don't know you in this mood,' she said, a little anxious. 'I think I prefer your arrogance . . . I know how to deal with that. Humility doesn't become you, Mr Duffy.'

'My name is Howard,' he pointed out sharply. 'Use it, girl!'

Tiffany chuckled, her spirits soaring. She did not know what would be the outcome of this sudden volte face. She did not know whether or not to believe his astounding claim that he loved her. But she did know that her misery at Kit's was at an end . . . that they could at least be friends in the future. Only time would tell if he really loved her—in the meantime she might be wise to tread softly where he was concerned, not to give too much of herself too soon, admit only that she liked him and would welcome a warmer understanding between them without betraying that she loved him so dearly and deeply. She could not bear to be hurt again by this man—and much as she loved him she did not know him very well. She knew that he could be cold and contemptuous and cruel . . . she knew that he could be tender and considerate and kind when he wished. But there were so many other things she wanted to know about him . . . and now, just when everything had seemed so hopeless and she had been on the verge of giving up the work she loved and enjoyed because of the heartache and humiliation he had caused her, it seemed that he was offering her the opportunity to find out those things, to discover if he was really the man she would love for the rest of her life and to ensure so that there was absolutely no doubt if he would love her and look after her as she longed and needed to be loved and cherished . . .

She held out her hands to him impulsively. 'Let's be friends, Howard,' she said warmly, appealingly.

He took her hands and carried them, first one then the other, to his lips. 'That will do to begin with,' he told her quietly. 'But I won't be content for long with just your friendship, Tiffany . . . I need your love and I'm determined to win it! I've never yet failed to get what I want in life—and I want you with all my heart!'

'Arrogant to the end!' she teased him gently.

'Not arrogant . . . just confident that I know where my happiness lies,' he amended—and he took her slowly, surely into his arms and held her close, his lips brushing her hair until, moved by an impulse, a need she could not control, Tiffany turned her head and sought his kiss. And she sighed a contented little sigh as their lips met and the sweetness and tenderness of his kiss erased all the heartache and unhappiness of the past, difficult weeks . . .

ROMANCE

Variety is the spice of romance

Each month, Mills & Boon publish new romances. New stories about people falling in love. A world of variety in romance – from the best writers in the romantic world. Choose from these titles in July.

PERHAPS LOVE Lindsay Armstrong
PAGAN ADVERSARY Sara Craven
NEVER SAY NEVER Claudia Jameson
FORBIDDEN WINE Lynsey Stevens
THE DEMETRIOUS LINE Margaret Pargeter
YESTERDAY'S ISLAND Anne Weale
ROSES AND CHAMPAGNE Betty Neels
HEAVEN HERE ON EARTH Carole Mortimer
NO ALTERNATIVE Margaret Way
LIGHTNING STRIKES TWICE Sue Peters
GALLANT ANTAGONIST Jessica Steele
SEEDS OF APRIL Celia Scott

On sale where you buy paperbacks. If you require further information or have any difficulty obtaining them, write to: Mills & Boon Reader Service, PO Box 236, Thornton Road, Croydon, Surrey CR9 3RU, England.

Mills & Boon
the rose of romance

Doctor Nurse Romances

Romance in modern medical life

Read more about the lives and loves of doctors and nurses in the fascinatingly different backgrounds of contemporary medicine. These are the four Doctor Nurse romances to look out for next month.

NURSE OVERBOARD
Meg Wisgate
EMERGENCY NURSE
Grace Read
DOCTORS IN DISPUTE
Jean Evans
WRONG DOCTOR JOHN
Kate Starr

Buy them from your usual paperback stockist, or write to: Mills & Boon Reader Service, P.O. Box 236, Thornton Rd, Croydon, Surrey CR9 3RU, England. Readers in South Africa-write to: Mills & Boon Reader Service of Southern Africa, Private Bag X3010, Randburg, 2125.

Mills & Boon
the rose of romance

Doctor Nurse Romances

Amongst the intense emotional pressures of modern medical life, doctors and nurses often find romance. Read about their lives and loves in the other three Doctor Nurse titles available this month.

DR VENABLES' PRACTICE
by Anne Vinton

The position of Nurse-Receptionist in Dr Laurence Venables' Harley Street practice is viewed with mixed feelings by Staff Nurse Penny Hunt. For, despite his extreme good looks, the distinguished Dr Venables makes her hackles rise – even when he isn't trying!

SHAMROCK NURSE
by Elspeth O'Brien

Nurse Nuala Kavanagh, sent to nurse Blake Wendover after the surgeon's eyes have been accidentally damaged, is as concerned as the rest of St.Jude's staff about his sight. Will she ever be more than a softly-voiced, gentle presence to him?

ICE VENTURE NURSE
by Lydia Balmain

Against the advice of Dr Kurt Rothwell, Sarah Barford is appointed nurse on the exploration trawler, *Ice Venture*. Trying to prove she is every bit as capable as a male nurse is almost impossible while the difficult Dr Rothwell is intent on proving his point . . .

Mills & Boon
the rose of romance

Fall in love – with

Do you remember the first time you fell in love? The heartache, the excitement, the happiness? Mills & Boon know – that's why they're the best-loved name in romantic fiction.

The world's finest romance authors bring to life the emotions, the conflicts and the joys of true love, and you can share them – between the covers of a Mills & Boon.

We are offering you the chance to enjoy Twelve specially selected Mills & Boon Romances absolutely FREE and without obligation. Take these free books and you will meet twelve women who must face doubt, fear and disappointment before discovering lasting love and happiness.

And with the help of the Mills & Boon Reader Service you could continue to receive the very latest Mills & Boon titles hot off the presses, delivered to your door each and every month.

Mills & Boon Reader Service, PO Box 236, Croydon, Surrey CR9 3RU.

NO STAMP NEEDED

To: Mills & Boon Reader Service, FREEPOST, PO Box 236, Croydon, Surrey CR9 9EL

Please send me, free and without obligation, twelve selected Mills & Boon Romances together with a current edition of the Newsletter, and reserve a Reader Service subscription for me. If I decide to subscribe I shall, from the beginning of the month following my free parcel of books, receive 12 new books each month for £11.40, post and packing free. If I decide not to subscribe, I shall write to you within 14 days, but whatever I decide the free books are mine to keep. I understand that I may cancel my subscription at any time simply by writing to you. I am over 18 years of age.

Please Write in BLOCK CAPITALS.

Name _____

Address _____

_____ Post Code _____

Offer applies in UK only. Overseas send for details. If price changes are necessary you will be notified.

SEND NO MONEY – TAKE NO RISKS

7D3T